"There are plenty of twists ahead . . . a triple-cross and (gangsters being what they are) perhaps one beyond that. It takes a lot of coincidences to occur for all of the pieces together, but as in the best of Cornell Woolrich, Fielding makes us believe them at the time."
—Steve Lewis, *Mystery*File*

Take Me As I Am
By Darwin Teilhet
Writing as
William H. Fielding

Black Gat Books • Eureka California

TAKE ME AS I AM

Published by Black Gat Books
A division of Stark House Press
1315 H Street
Eureka, CA 95501, USA
griffinskye3@sbcglobal.net
www.starkhousepress.com

TAKE ME AS I AM
Published by Gold Medal Books and copyright © 1952 by Fawcett
Publications, Inc., New York, as by "William H. Fielding."

All rights reserved under International and Pan-American Copyright
Conventions.

ISBN: 979-8-88601-029-9

Cover and text design by Jeff Vorzimmer, ¡caliente!design, Austin, Texas

PUBLISHER'S NOTE:
This is a work of fiction. Names, characters, places and incidents are either
the products of the author's imagination or used fictionally, and any
resemblance to actual persons, living or dead, events or locales, is entirely
coincidental.

Without limiting the rights under copyright reserved above, no part of this
publication may be reproduced, stored, or introduced into a retrieval system
or transmitted in any form or by any means (electronic, mechanical,
photocopying, recording or otherwise) without the prior written permission of
both the copyright owner and the above publisher of the book.

First Stark House Press/Black Gat Edition: May 2023

Chapter One

About sunrise that Saturday morning the green Nash drove west from the town of Boone, cruising along slowly for an hour, before it circled around to the south to enter the old quarry road from the east.

Everything had been timed. Tires whined eagerly, like dogs on a fresh scent. Pinkey was driving. Monk was on the right-hand side, waiting with the stovepipe, the bazooka. A third man was in the back seat. It was a small mob. It was a real small mob for a real big heist, Monk was thinking. But the stovepipe was a technological booster for a small mob. That was what Gramma once had said. *The technological booster*. Monk liked that. He really did.

When the armored pay truck was sighted, Pinkey gunned the Nash close to ninety in the final spurt. He swung out to pass. Inside the Nash, Monk saw only a blurred impression of something like an enormous gray beetle on wheels. It was happening so fast those guys in that pay truck still hadn't got the idea something was going to bust at them in another forty-five seconds. Monk braced himself for Pinkey to slam on the brakes. But right then the man in the Nash's rear seat gave quick warning.

Monk had also seen the danger. Ahead of the armored pay truck, pacing it, rode a state cop on a motorcycle. That cop hadn't been anticipated by Gramma. Monk saw Pinkey's face turn slightly, his mouth working, asking for instructions. All in a flash Monk had to decide.

He lunged, big and bulky, shouting to the man humped in the back seat to take out that copper.

Immediately Pinkey clamped on the foot brakes and the Nash careened violently, tailing back and forth on the narrow road and leaving a trail of rubbery smoke from the tires. It stopped sideways across the road.

Monk was pitched forward. But the man in the back seat was good. It was all over in split seconds. His machine gun muzzle smashed the rear window even before the car had fully stopped, and as Monk got out he heard the chopping racket.

Halfway between the clumsy armed truck and the Nash, the state cop began falling apart. The motorcycle wobbled. Its engine roared against the staccato racket from the Nash. A front wheel suddenly crumpled, and a chain unwound like a snake. The cop fell backward, with little red tufts all at once sprouting from him like small feathers; he struck the road and he stayed there.

Monk was swearing, the same dull word over and over again. He pulled frantically at a big tube which looked something like a stovepipe. Leaning into the front of the car, his back and legs were exposed; any second he expected lead from those bums in the armored truck. Pinkey had leaped out on the other side, firing deliberately and carefully with the big service forty-five. Now Chopper Boy was on the pavement, too, giving the truck a long burst. Monk pulled the stovepipe from the Nash. Although he'd rehearsed it time and time again during six stinking months of waiting until finally he could load within three seconds, now it took him a damned extra second longer because his hands were sweaty and seemed all thumbs.

He shoved the charge into the stovepipe. He had turn, kneeling on the road. He lifted the stovepipe, feeling one end of the barrel pressing coldly against his ear and running behind his head to carry the blast away from him. He took another second to sight through the cross wires, bringing the armored truck into center.

For this continuing second he was all alone on this side of the Nash and he'd never felt so exposed. He couldn't see Pinkey or Chopper Boy. They were hidden from him on the opposite side of the Nash. They'd probably fallen flat on the pavement to protect themselves. He felt rage against them because right now he had to show himself to the men in the armored truck.

But the air had become hideous from the Chopper's spraying, even if machine gun bullets didn't do much more than dent an armored pay truck at that distance. The state cop was still sprawled in the highway, not moving. The motorcycle had compressed itself into a shining ripple of tubes and wheels.

Everything between himself and the pay truck were only blurred details, scarcely seen. He was concentrating on the truck, three hundred and ten feet distant, approximately, by the calibered sights of the M3 old-style bazooka.

The armored truck had stopped. But just as Gramma had anticipated, the driver and guards inside were too confident. Instead of trying to turn around on the quarry road and run for it, they'd decided they could safely shoot it out behind the bullet-proof glass and the armor plate. Someone inside that truck had even had time to run out a machine gun through the nickel-plated orifice on the right-hand side of the glass windshield.

Through the cross wires Monk saw the machine gun poke its nozzle around left to right to stutter dimly at Pinkey and Chopper Boy on the other side of the Nash.

Monk's fingers jerked convulsively. He was rocked by the concussion, the blast spurting behind him. A red flower opened where the armored truck had been. The flower blossomed into a crashing of sound. Monk whirled, grabbing a second charge from the yellow box inside the Nash. He began running toward the smoking truck. The truck's machine gun was silenced. It could mean the four men inside the truck had been finished by the first explosion, but Monk didn't want to take any chances. He saw Pinkey was running along with him and had a moment of increased fury because he didn't see Chopper Boy. What the hell was he doing, staying behind?

After the explosion, the front end of the gray armored truck fell forward on the broken front wheels, its hood ripped off, its windshield shattered, with a man in uniform hanging head down into the engine's wreckage. The driver was still upright, clenching the steering wheel, but not much of his head remained. That accounted for two of them. But the two remaining guards could still be alive and waiting inside the rear of the truck.

Monk yelled, "Hold it, Pinkey," stopped before he got too close, and this time aimed at the right-hand side of the truck. The second explosion sent pieces of steel plate into the air like scraps of cardboard, and a whole fountain of smoke lifted. A burst of hot air kicked at Monk and he staggered, squinting his eyes, trying to see through the smoke. His eyes had been going bad on him. He needed his glasses but he couldn't risk wearing glasses on a job like this because glasses helped identify a man. Pinkey jumped in, ready to fire with his forty-five at anything that moved. Now Monk saw the third guard had been catapulted to the pavement, lying there like a sack, stone dead, the face a red ooze and eyeless.

Pinkey called, "O.K., Monk. There ain't enough of the fourth boy to scrape up."

Monk threw down the bazooka, its usefulness was ended. That was part of the rehearsed plan. Leave everything unnecessary, Gramma had said patiently, over and over again. The bazooka couldn't be traced. Gramma had seen to that. Monk wedged his big bulky body through the jagged opening in the side of the truck, and his nearsighted eyes now saw what Pinkey meant by saying the fourth boy couldn't even be scraped up. That fixed it good. Nobody left to finger them.

The metal floor of the truck was pitched at an angle because the second shot from the bazooka had smashed a rear wheel as well as tearing out half of the outer wall. Although the old 1942 issues had long since been replaced by the army's heavier and more accurate tank killers, it had taken somebody with Gramma's brains to see one of the old-style bazookas still packed all the firepower needed to smash open any pay truck.

Monk saw the fiber suitcase. Of course it wasn't really a fiber suitcase. It was a regulation Federal reserve shipment case. But Gramma had always been careful, even to the smallest details. It had made it easier for Monk to know instantly what he was looking for by saying it looked like a fiber suitcase. It had fallen along the slant of floor and was hanging there, the chain still attached by the regulation padlock. Monk hauled out his thirty-eight special. A sudden doubt flickered in his mind—could a case that small hold half a million dollars? Monk took few more seconds to peer around the crumpled interior. No, by God. This was the only case. This was it, all right.

He heard Pinkey's worried snarl, "Geez, Monk, we're losing too much time!"

Monk shot at the chain. One shot should have been enough since the chain end was only stapled into the hard fiber. But Monk was shooting from an awkward position. The second shot snapped the chain free from the case. He backed out into the morning light. He saw Pinkey waiting but he didn't see Chopper Boy. All at once he had vague intimation of something perhaps having gone off the track. But he had no time for much thinking. Everything was too silent and still after the gunfire and explosions.

In the silence, Pinkey's voice sounded too loud. "We're running behind time, Monk. Suppose that doll of yours gets tired waiting in the transfer car? You got the stuff?"

Monk nodded. He had the stuff. What the hell did Pinkey think was in this fiber case? Pinkey was always asking unnecessary questions. He could drive a car down a rat hole if he had to and that was why Gramma had picked him, but when he wasn't behind a steering wheel he yakked too much. Monk swung his chunky head around in a final quick check-up. The road remained empty. For a second he still could persuade himself everything had gone smoothly.

But Pinkey was saying something, pointing north toward a cornfield. A lane ran through the field, higher above the field, to a farmhouse. Monk squinted. Perhaps a quarter of a mile away, two people were running toward the road. They'd heard the shooting and explosions. The dopes lacked the sense God gave them to keep out of it, he thought.

Monk told Pinkey, "Pick them off if you can, but hurry," and started running toward the Nash, the fiber bag banging against his left leg. Behind him he heard three hard slamming sounds from Pinkey's forty-five. He didn't look behind him or toward the cornfield. If he felt anything he felt anger because a couple of jerks from a farm hadn't had the sense to stay inside just two more minutes. But all he really was thinking of was to get back to the Nash and drive it like hell to where his transfer was waiting.

Because he was the big joe on this job he had to carry the hot money on through the final stage. Not until he got rid of the hot money, with nothing on him any more to prove he'd been in this caper, would he be able to relax a little and have the swarm of bees inside his blood stream gradually melt away.

He pounded past the dead copper. Pinkey wasn't far behind. All at once Monk stopped short, his breath exhaling. Crumpled on the road not far from the left rear wheel of the Nash was Chopper Boy. It was the face of an old chopper boy, a real old one, about forty. Four holes were drilled straight across the flat forehead.

Pinkey said, "I didn't have no chance to tell you. They get him jus' when you aimed the stovepipe."

"The sonsabitches."

Until three hours ago Monk had never even seen this particular chopper boy. But he was part of the mob. He had been allied with Monk. Those armored truck guards had had no right to kill him, Monk felt, not aware of his grotesque reasoning. The boy was dead, stinking dead. But before the caper Gramma had had the foresight to have all three of his boys wear old clothes from which all identification marks had been removed.

"We don't take him, do we, boy?" Pinkey said.

"We just leave him here," Monk said. "Get going."

More shrilly Pinkey explained that the two farmers had hidden in their house. Phone wires were strung to it. That meant a phone. But there wasn't time now to get back to that telephone pole and cut the connecting wires to that farmhouse. Monk slammed the door on his side, immediately being thrown against the seat as Pinkey gunned the ignition.

Monk could trust Pinkey with the driving. For the next fifteen minutes or so it was Pinkey's responsibility to get the two of them to the first transfer point. The big purring rumble from the engine was vaguely reassuring. Monk held the money case on his knees. The lock had been smashed. His fingers began prying at the lid.

In his mind he tried to calculate a problem of time and distance. Those jerks in the farmhouse would probably phone the police or the sheriff's office at Boone, which was some four miles east of the quarry road. Well, there was still a margin. It wasn't such a fat margin as Gramma had so confidently believed; still, it ought to be ample. As soon as Monk reached the transfer car and could ditch these damned greasy rags and get into decent clothes again and put the money case out of sight, even if a longer stage followed before final delivery, it would be progressively easier and easier. It was right now when he was out of action and it depended on Pinkey that the swarm of bees inside his veins became intolerable.

He got the lid open and suddenly felt his throat swell with the soundless gushing of more rage. The case was packed with flat bundles of bank notes, all right. But he was saved the trouble of having to count them. It was all there for him to see, the typewritten list, done in triplicate, the total added, properly signed with unknown signatures. According to the list this shipment contained twenty-five bundles of twenty-dollar notes, two thousand to each bundle; twenty-five of tens, one thousand a bundle; and five of fifties, five thousand each. The total was one hundred thousand dollars.

While that wasn't hay, as a fresh young punk might say, Monk began saying one dull curse over and over again Out of the corner of his mouth Pinkey asked thinly "Ain't we got it?" Monk told him. They'd stuck their necks into it for a puking hundred thousand when they had assumed it would be for a half million.

This was only a stinking regular mixed shipment from the reserve to the branch bank at Boone. Mixed shipments came through every week in various denominations. For six months Gramma had been patiently waiting until one of the big shipments was scheduled to be sent through. This, presumably, had been the morning.

Gramma's cut was half. That was standard. For half the profits, Gramma planned the jig, paid expenses, and even if it was understood that he remained in the background he had a reputation of standing by his boys through trouble, with a big mouthpiece appearing out of nowhere and all the defense money required. In return, his boys all knew what happened if they failed to stand by Gramma.

As big joe on this one Monk was to have a quarter slice. The final piece of pie would be a two-way split between Pinkey and Chopper Boy, who was now past caring. For the almost certain take of half a million, Monk had considered his cut of $125,000 worth risking the really big trouble. With slightly bulging eyes he stared at the neat packets of new bank notes. Pinkey had taken it equally hard, saying soft wretched words. He turned into another road, and another at the next four corners. He was behind time for the pick-up but he was too good a driver to drive too fast and risk attracting attention to the Nash from the scattering of cars passing by.

Monk said, "A stinking hundred grand!"

Without turning his head, Pinkey said, "Gramma ain't gonna like hearing he got the wrong tip-off."

Monk was thinking he wasn't going to like having to tell Alma it was only a hundred grand. She'd come into this, as he had, for the one chance of really big money.

"One thing," Pinkey said more hopefully, "Chopper Boy won't want his cut no more. That gives me and you an extra slice."

Monk said thickly what he thought of that thin extra slice. Sweat came out on him like drops of blood from the swarm of bees inside him. Pinkey's head nodded. They were all gypped. Now they had to keep on, whether they liked it or not. Monk couldn't help thinking that it would be at least a little better if Pinkey and he just kept Gramma's fifty-grand cut. Next, he thought of the big trouble that from now on would always be waiting somewhere as long as he lived. He'd need Gramma. He couldn't do without Gramma. It would be rough not to know Gramma also was there, ready to do all possible to shield the boys, providing the boys broke no rules.

So he didn't say anything about leaving out Gramma; and neither did Pinkey, although perhaps the same nervous greedy thoughts slid through his narrow head. Pinkey ran the Nash around a curve. A kind of hollow stretched ahead of them where probably guys hunted ducks in the fall. He said, "Here we are, boy," bringing the Nash to an easy stop. He looked back and then forward. At least here their luck was good. No other cars were in sight. Monk closed the money case, opening the door.

Pinkey grinned mirthlessly. "Boy, it's all yours. Me, I'd ruther git a small cut than a big slice an' have to deliver hot money. Tell Gramma I'll be around. See you, boy. See you . . ."

All at once Pinkey was shoving the Nash away, smooth and fast but not too fast to attract attention. From now on all Pinkey had to do was to get safely somewhere by himself in the Nash long enough to change into new clothes and get rid of the clothes he was wearing. After that, even if he was halted it would be next to impossible to prove he'd had a hand in the jig back there. It was the big joe with the hot money who remained so hot he could smell himself cooking until finally he completed delivery.

Monk began running. He stumbled, fell heavily, got up, grabbed the money case, and ran for his life. He crawled over a fence and still ran after he was out of sight from the road. The ground became soggy. Old willows lifted, their greenness shading away the morning sunlight and at last Monk got control of his panic. He found the wagon trail leading through the willow grove and walked south on the trail, his lungs having a sensation of turning into rancid butter. He was late. He knew that. But he didn't know how many minutes late because he wasn't carrying a watch. He wasn't carrying anything in these shabby clothes which ever could give him away. However, when he sighted worriedly through the green leaves the sun seemed much too high in the sky.

He started running again. He saw the blue Plymouth, half hidden between a willow and the rotting frame of an empty farmhouse. Instead of staying there, though, the Plymouth was receding from him. He shouted. She had given him up. The tramp! He could see himself being left here while a circle would be tightening hour by hour around him. Even if the willow grove had been selected in advance as the one temporarily secure place for the first transfer, it would be only a matter of time before sheriffs or farmers deputized and carrying shotguns began slowly walking down through the willows.

He called desperately, "Alma! Alma!"

All at once the Plymouth did stop. She'd heard him. He began running toward the Plymouth. The trim schoolgirl inside the Plymouth thrust her neat head through the window to look back at him, and Monk felt his knees buckle under him. It wasn't Alma, after all. It was some high-school or college girl who must have parked here, perhaps waiting for her fellow. Now what was he going to do? With an arm he wiped sweat from his eyes, realizing exactly what he was going to have to do.

Chapter Two

She had waited there, watching the minutes go by on her wrist watch. Fear increased. It was fourteen minutes past the time. Fifteen minutes. Sixteen. The trees seemed to be moving closer and closer toward her every time she looked around. Seventeen minutes! She didn't know what had happened. Monk might have been killed.

High in the morning sky a bird cried piercingly. Suddenly, all she could think of was to get out of here, quickly. In her mounting panic, she flooded the carburetor. At last the motor caught on. The Plymouth bumped violently over the old forgotten lane.

Far behind, someone was shouting. She was afraid to stop. She knew a cop or sheriff was there. But she had to look back. It was Monk! Oh, God! Weak with relief, she pushed on the brake, killing the engine. He ran heavily to the Plymouth, his mouth all hanging open and his face as white as a dead fish. His eyes bulged at her. He had a case like a suitcase in his left hand and his right hand was bringing up a gun. "Monk!" she cried.

Again a bird screamed high in the sky. Slowly, he shoved the gun into his pocket and said, "What you done to yourself, kid? I nearly didn't know you."

"Nothing, honey. Nothing much. I just stopped looking so much like a tramp. Oh, God, Monk. I got so scared when you didn't come. What went wrong?"

"You tramp—" His own face began coming back together again. "Nothing's wrong. We got it. That dope, Pink, was slow getting here, that's all."

Suppose he'd been delayed another two or three minutes until she'd driven so far she couldn't hear him calling? She deserved a beating. She waited for him to go around the car. She had nearly failed him. She was no good when the pressure was on. She'd always known that. She tried to smile at him as he climbed heavily into the Plymouth, sitting beside her and dropping the fiber case between his legs.

"Monk, honey," she said, wanting to say she hadn't meant to run off on him.

"Get going," he ordered.

She'd half expected him to hit her. She got going. She could ask him all the questions later. No, she didn't want to know too much. The less she knew, the better. All that money would be in that case down there on the rubber floorboard. It was wonderful how a bank could pack so much money into such a small case. Half a million dollars!

Monk was undressing. She heard him grunt as he leaned forward, unlacing his shoes. He had to strip everything he'd worn on the job and get into brand new clothes, all new from the skin out. Later, if by chance he was picked up on suspicion, the nosies wouldn't find any particles of dust or mud or burnt powder or—her mind refused consciously to think, blood—or anything. All this infinite attention to details was wonderfully reassuring. The Plymouth moved past the deserted farmhouse, a blackened shell of barn, and into a green marshy country where the great feathery willows lifted high on either side of the old trail.

She let the car crawl along in low gear, but every mile forward through the big willow marsh was better than ten along open country roads. She didn't know who had reconnoitered the lane through the willow trees, to report that it was dry and solid enough by now for a car to get through.

She didn't want to know. That part of it hadn't concerned her. Next to her, Monk had stripped himself down to the skin. He wrapped the old shoes inside the shabby work clothes which he had worn for the job, the heavy rubber gloves still sheathing his hands and wrists.

He said, "What was you running off from me for, kid?"

"I waited. Honest. But I—I—"

"I guess I was kinda late," he said. "Well, to hell with it."

She had to ask one question. "You got the money?"

"All the pay wagon had."

All that money! And Monk wasn't too sore because she'd gone chicken and started to pull out. Oh, God, what a sweet guy he was. Everything he was saying, had gone one, two, three. Those gas bombs had been what the doctor ordered.

Months ago when he'd first explained about the job he had told her that Gramma was much too smart to risk any killing. It was like this, see? Gramma had got hold of some gas bombs. And because she had wanted so very much to have her hands on Monk's two-hundred-and-fifty-thousand piece of pie, she had nodded her head. Gas bombs exploded. Guards and driver in the armored truck breathed in all those fumes and just sort of passed out for a few hours. Although she was too intelligent not to have a doubt, with her it was a little like hearing a noise downstairs in the middle of a dark night and deciding just to let it go.

It was always better when something began troubling you, just to let it go, anyway. Sometimes unpleasant things just happened. If you held on to them, thinking too much, a girl might end some morning with somebody finding her hanging from one of her stockings. Alma shivered. Monk was here. He had a whole case jammed with money. That was all that was really important.

Her mind went off at random while Monk was saying Chopper Boy and Pinkey were sure to be safe by now. The thing couldn't miss. Gramma had planned it too good. She could see herself in a week or so strolling around Cuba, with Monk, or maybe in Hawaii or maybe even in Italy.

She was beginning to feel much safer. She despised herself for nearly breaking and running out back there. In another mile or more they'd have passed through the willow marsh to be just two people in new vacation clothes driving along a country road in a nice new Plymouth.

Monk asked, "Where's my stuff?"

"In back. In the tire compartment."

"My glasses?"

"Everything's there, honey."

"Cigars?"

She said brightly, "Everything," although she hoped Monk would quit smoking those ten-cent stinkers now they were really in the big money. He ought to try a pipe. He'd look good with a pipe, like those men in advertisements.

"Let's stop here," he said. "It looks safe."

She did have a feeling of them being secure and hidden within the big willows. She waited while Monk dug a big hole in the soft ground with the car's emergency shovel. After dropping the bundle into the hole he pulled off the rubber gloves, threw them in, filled the hole with moist earth, tamped it, and scraped rotting leaves and moss over the earth with his bare feet. Deliberately she let her eyes seek to him. The sight of him distracted her. It helped push down inside her mind the bad part people like Monk and her had to accept if ever they were going to get anywhere.

All right. So Monk had helped to knock over a pay truck. Honestly! What about what you read day after day in the newspapers? Those people in Washington were the big crooks. They were really crooked. They got millions without ever risking themselves as Monk had, taking his chances. They never got caught. Nobody lifted a hand to stop them. They got theirs. They got plenty and nobody cared. Why shouldn't Monk and she get a little on their own? That pay truck was insured. Nobody got badly hurt. Well, all right, she thought, surprised. Of a sudden she was angry and unsure and thinking too much about it. Well, my gracious! Heavens! She had to remind herself she was finished swearing like a little no-good tramp.

Sweat was shining on his broad heavy shoulders. He stood there, looking at her. She looked back, grinning a little. He passed around to the rear, opened the trunk and put away the shovel, and returned with a shabby leather bag initialed "A.J."

From the bag he removed a tweed coat, slacks, a silk tie, everything a man needed, tossing all but the shoes and socks on the seat beside her. He used the towel in the bag to wipe himself off carefully, from the shoulders down, taking time with his legs and feet before putting on socks and shoes. Instead of getting in to finish dressing, though, he turned, standing framed by the open door as she let herself look at him. She saw the hard chest with its black hair, the belly traced by hair around the navel, the tapering hips and sturdy legs.

Admiringly, Monk asked, "What you done to yourself all these months, Alma? Jesus, I hardly knowed you that first sight. I was expectin' to see my flashy yella-haired doll. When Gramma sees you he's gunna think I stole some babe fresh outa some convent."

She was answering, but all the time she was watching his body and remembering that time when the hired man had put the boar into the pen with her mamma's new sow. The memory of it came and vanished all within an instant. . . .

She had been fourteen or fifteen, then. It wasn't so long ago, either, not more than seven years ago. Her father had been killed in a coal mine. She was old enough to realize her mother wasn't quite like the other kids' mothers who lived in the neighborhood. Her mother hadn't been born in this country; her mother was only about thirty-five and looked younger, and she was trying to run a fifteen-acre produce farm with the help of a big-boned blond fellow of twenty or so whom she paid by the day.

Once or twice a month he stayed for supper. After supper he remained in the kitchen to help her mother with the accounts and Alma was sent to bed early. His name was Dale. Alma had a crush on him. It made her mad as anything because she was always sent to bed early on those nights as if she were still a little kid.

It seemed terribly unfair. She wanted to stay down in the kitchen and hear Dale tell of all the big cities he'd seen. Alma had a vision of herself as she'd been seven or eight years ago, her hair in those stupid long braids her mother said young girls had to have, when Alma no longer considered herself a young girl, probably gawky-looking, but grown as tall as she was now, and wearing one of those flower-bag dresses with nothing underneath.

It was an afternoon in the middle of summer. In a few days Dale was going into the Army. She might never see him again. He was grinning at her, taking her hand and leading her behind the barn to show her how the neighbor's boar he'd borrowed could really make up to her mama's new sow.

Of course she knew all about such things. When you were born and brought up on a farm it was commonplace, only after you began to get older sometimes you'd giggle about it with the kids. But she had never thought about it as anything so terribly unusual until Dale began whispering to her and kind of pestering her that Saturday while her mamma was in town buying seed. It was different, too, watching with Dale after the boar was let into the pen with the sow.

Even if she knew it was being wicked she hadn't ever known anything could be so exciting to watch when somebody like Dale was there with you, whispering and whispering. It gave her such a limp breathless feeling she let Dale push her against the barn. Dale was saying something. She shook her head. Then he was whispering again. Her throat contracted so tight she couldn't speak. She felt his hand, lifting her dress, and suddenly he had his arms around her and she was clinging to him. All that time he had been her hero and had never noticed her, and now he knew she wasn't a little girl any more.

She was trembling like a leaf. She still remembered that first time. Even more, she remembered that when she raised her head she saw her mamma over there by the fence. She didn't know how long her mamma had been there. She didn't think Dale did, either, for suddenly he was saying loud frightened words to her mamma. Alma didn't want to listen. She ran like a young doe. When she was on the other side of the barn she heard a shot, followed by a second, from the double-barreled shotgun her mamma had been holding. She yelled, "Ma! Ma!" There was no reply. Cautiously, she slipped around the barn. Next, she was screaming at the top of her lungs. It was all of seven years ago but she had never forgotten the sight of Dale and her mamma lying there in the dust.

She was speaking very fast to Monk. She wanted him to understand she was finished wearing those frilly clothes and that green suit she used to wear, with her hair falling halfway down her back. In the long months of waiting she'd decided she wanted to look like college girls looked. She'd quit giving her hair that flashy yellow rinse, too. So she was a natural blonde, wasn't she? So a real natural blonde was really a kind of pale blondish brown, not a bright yellow. She hoped Monk liked having her hair back to this natural blonde shade, honey.

But her voice had faltered.

Monk had shoved all the new clothes he was supposed to wear to one side. He sat next to her. He was big and hairy and she could smell his smell. In some of the ways that counted he wasn't like Dale. But Dale had been dead for over seven years.

She wriggled over on the car seat and ran her lips over his shoulder. "Monk, honey."

He just sat there.

She leaned back. "What's the matter, honey?"

"I'm too pooped from that job. I can't. Keep thinkin' of that money."

Suddenly she hated him. She snapped her teeth together like a she-fox. All he could think about was that hot money. She felt soiled. She smoothed her skirt. She hated him even more bitterly because later he would want to fondle her and make love to her. He'd failed her. After all she'd been through for him, and just when she was—Money! He was only half a man. She hated him and she hated herself.

Monk finished dressing, saying, "You drive kid. I'm real pooped. How do I look?"

She started the Plymouth, glancing at him. That tweed coat looked expensive. The gray slacks were well cut and probably of English flannel. She knew he was supposed to give the impression of being a young business executive out for a drive in the country. But he had gained weight, she noticed. In another few years if he wasn't careful he was going to turn flabby. That tie he was wearing kind of screamed at you, though. It didn't go with the rest of his outfit. It was hand painted with a sort of swirl of tiny little figures of girls romping against a bright green pattern on the silk; and, while she'd seen fancy hand painted ties that almost knocked out your eyes, this one, she thought, really took the brass ring. "Where'd you get that tie, Monk?"

"What's wrong with it? Gramma got it where he buys all the clothes for his boys. At Crabtree's, I heard, the best store in Omaha. I told you, didn't I, that Gramma likes his mob to dress good when they ain't on jobs."

"That's a good-looking coat and slacks," she admitted. "But that tie doesn't go so good. If a motorcycle cop rides by and happens to take a look in at us, that tie's going to flash his eyes. I don't think you ought to wear anything anybody might remember you by, do you? Look at me. I quit looking so hot stuff. I don't even have make-up on this morning."

"Maybe you got something, kid."

Monk yanked off his tie and stuffed it behind him, between the seat cushion and the back of the seat. "I don't like anything around my throat, anyway."

"Like a rope?" Alma said.

"That ain't so funny. Lay off them cracks. Just git goin'."

After she reached the country road some of the compression inside her started easing off. She liked having the fiber case packed with all that money on the floor where she could stick her foot on it if she wished.

Who was going to stop them now? The armored truck had been knocked off, miles away, near Boone. There weren't enough available cops or sheriffs to try to search every car on every road in the state. No, the coppers would still be nosing around inside one of those ten-or fifteen-mile area circles as they always did right after a heist job. It was all coppers could do. If you got out of the area circle in time the rest of it ought to be easy.

Monk slumped low in the seat. He did look terribly tired, she thought. "I guess right now I'm too pooped to think. I'll sack off. That job took more outa me than I thought. You watch it?"

"I'll watch it, honey," she said. "Don't worry."

"Don't drive too fast. We don't wanta be picked up for speedin' or nothin', not with the fresh case of green goods."

She watched it. The Plymouth had traveled a good seventy-eight miles toward the final delivery place when Monk aroused himself. He asked where they were. Alma answered, "In a few minutes we'll be on the main highway, west, honey."

"I sure feel pooped, Alma. Nothing over the radio yet?"

"I guess I didn't think to listen."

"Alma—" there was even more of a slumped heaviness about him. "I better tell you—I didn't make out so good."

She didn't understand.

"It's like this. Alma. We only got a hundred grand. That was all the armored truck carried, kid. It didn't have half a million."

Only a hundred thousand? Monk's quarter slice would only be twenty-five thousand. *Twenty-five thousand!* It was like a knife stab. Monk was supposed to get one hundred and twenty-five thousand as his share of the job. Damn it to hell! Tears stung her eyes. It was so unfair. She wouldn't even have Monk's piddling little cut out of the heist either. She'd tailed in, depending on him to be generous.

"Monk," she said without thinking. "Why cut in Gramma? Why don't we keep the whole hundred thousand?"

He cuffed her across the cheek.

"Shut upl Don't ever say that. You hear? Don't even think it. You know how Gramma is."

"I—was just kidding." Her cheek burned from Monk's rasping palm.

"Gramma don't take that kind of kidding. You never saw him shoot flies offa wall with his pistol, didja? You can't kid with Gramma."

She had met Gramma only once, six months ago. It still chilled her to think of that elephantine man with the gray wrinkled face. Monk leaned forward, fiddling with the radio. She had never thought that Monk would be so easily scared, though, by Gramma and Gramma's pistols. If Monk had guts, she stubbornly told herself, he'd take that hundred thousand and let Gramma root for it. She would. She was in so deep now, anyway, what did it matter if Gramma was cut out of it? With a hundred thousand dollars, at least you'd have your one chance to try to get away, so far away you might even learn to be decent and nice and sort of sassy like those college girls back in Des Moines.

Monk had turned on the 11:30 news broadcast. The voice was giving the weather report and farm prices. With a hundred thousand dollars, she was thinking, Monk and she could get so far away you wouldn't hear newscasts that began always with a weather report and the latest farm prices. Now the voice was telling about the armored car that had been blown up early this morning a few miles outside Boone. Alma began having a sick feeling. Monk hadn't said anything to her about using one of those Army bazookas. Oh, God! A state patrol officer killed, the driver of the armored car, the three guards, one of the gangsters . . .

Next the voice said, "The fourth guard, John Kennilly, although left for dead on the pavement, did not die until a few hours later in the Mercy hospital. The explosion had blinded him. All honor and credit must go to this courageous man. Wracked by pain, he lay there, not stirring, allowing these thugs to believe he was dead. He heard one speak to the other, calling him 'Monk.' He lived long enough to report that to the police officers. He also reported a woman was driving the transfer car.

"Ladies and gentlemen! A flash has just come in. Sheriff Howard Rittenhouse, in co-operation with the FBI and the Milwaukee police department, now believes the leader of these gangsters was Monk Anzeiger. Repeat, Monk Anzeiger—well-known Milwaukee hoodlum and gunman. He disappeared last year from Milwaukee when wanted for questioning in regard to thefts of Army property, including two nineteen-forty-three-issue bazookas. All police officers have been asked to co-operate within an area extending west to the state line, north to Fort Dodge, east to Grinnel, and south to Creston. Somewhere within this area Monk Anzeiger is either in hiding or trying to get out of the state in a car driven by an unidentified woman. The description of Monk Anzeiger is as follows: Thirty-six years old, about two hundred and ten pounds, swarthy faced, black hair, bald on top, known to wear glasses . . ."

Monk cut off the radio. "That damn Pinkey," he said. "He talked too much. We thought the fella on the pavement was smeared. Pinkey said to hurry because we were behind time getting me to the babe in the transfer car. At least Pinkey never mentioned your name or the kinda car."

"Monk," she said faintly. "I gotta stop. I gotta."

She was sick behind the bushes. She hadn't known, she told herself. She hadn't. It was such a perfect setup, nobody even getting hurt because of the gas bombs. She wanted to run. She wanted to get away from Monk. She wasn't in it. Monk would burn if he was caught. She'd go to the cops. She'd say it wasn't her fault. She hadn't known. Then she saw Monk watching her from the car. If she started running she wouldn't get as far as the fence before he blasted her down. Her legs were like water.

He took over the wheel. The Plymouth ran smoothly along the road but all at once she knew everything was ending for them both. Right now it was like being in the dead center of a cyclone. What could they do? They couldn't go on or they'd run into a road block. They couldn't just stop. Monk surprised her by suddenly twisting the Plymouth off into a side lane and stopping.

"What are we going to do?" she cried. "Try to run?"

"Lissen. We're stuck. We gotta think fast. I'll burn on this if we're caught."

"Dump out the hot money!"

"Shut up. You're crazy. Throwin' out that dough won't save me from burnin' if I get caught. If we can get that dough to Gramma he's got to stick by us and help us to save his skin, don't he? Think of something."

"Gas bombs," she said viciously.

"You knew I was horsing. Say, lissen, Alma. I got it. I hide till tonight. *You* take the money to Gramma."

"Just great."

"No, lissen. If Gramma gets that dough he can't let us down. See that culvert over there? Through them pine trees. I can hide there, easy. I'll burrow down in old leaves and grass till midnight. Just tell Gramma that. Remember this place. He'll know how to get some of his boys through to pick me up."

"Monk, you fool. The coppers'll stop me."

"Lissen, will you? Use your head. Maybe they'll stop cars. They ain't gonna take time to search every damn car passing, are they? You're just some college girl driving through. You got the looks. You can sweet talk through," he said eagerly.

"Sure. I sweet talk and a copper sees that money case there," she said, pointing.

"Don't be like that. Here . . ."

She could smell his sweat. He pulled down the shabby leather case from the shelf behind him. He stuck it between Alma and him, wrenched it open, picked up the fiber case from the floor and lifted the top, which came free from the smashed lock. With savage haste he began cramming wads and wads of new bank notes into the leather case. A hundred thousand dollars! Alma felt her heart nearly stop.

"There!" Monk shoved the leather bag back behind them. He opened the door on his side, tucking the fiber case under an arm.

"I'll get rid of this empty case, kid."

"Monk—" He was leaving her. She was struck by panic.

"Lissen. Just do as I say. You'll make it."

"Where'll I find Gramma? You never told me."

"Drive straight to Atlantic. That's the next town. It ain't too far, only twenty or thirty miles. Probably you won't even be stopped. If you are, sweet talk. You'll get by. Your looks'll do it. You'll be just a college kid. Get to Atlantic. There's a little blue and red grocery store near the railroad station. You can't miss it. Gramma'll be waiting there. That's all you gotta do, kid. It's for me."

He gave her no time to protest. He jumped out and waved. "Get goin'," he called and then ran into the trees.

Her mind had the sensation of twisting frantically back and forth through a maze. There was no way out for her. She was certain to be caught. She knew she'd be caught. She started the Plymouth. When despairingly she tried to catch a last glimpse of Monk, he had vanished.

Each new mile increased the torture. It was nearly noon. A sprinkle of rain lashed streaks on the windshield. She had never felt so alone and exposed. She was faint with fear. She could imagine herself blacking out all of a sudden, in a crises of nerves, the Plymouth plunging off the road.

She had never expected it to be like this when months ago Monk had talked her into joining the job. Why hadn't Monk stayed with her? She couldn't drive much farther. The sick feeling was renewing itself in the pit of her stomach. She was strung to the breaking point, any second expecting to see a road block waiting ahead for her.

She tensed even at the sight of somebody walking along the highway. It was only a hitchhiker, a rangy youngster with tow-colored hair wet by the sprinkle, thumbing for a ride. He was waiting forty yards or so beyond, while the distance between him and the car diminished.

He looked like a big, nice country kid. Probably, she thought suddenly, a kid like that could drive a car. His hair was even lighter in color than her own. Something flashed through her mind. The alarm had gone out for an unidentified woman, who could be of any age and description, and a man of Monk's description, thirty-six, two hundred and ten pounds, black hair, bald on top, and wearing glasses. That big tow-headed kid waiting ahead for a ride, she saw, as the Plymouth approached, couldn't be over twenty. He was dressed in an old Army windbreaker, a wool shirt open at the neck, and corduroy pants, and a knapsack hung over his shoulder.

She felt a surging of hope. She began applying the brakes. If that big kid was driving with her any copper who flagged down the Plymouth might give the two of them only a casual glance before waving them on. She slowed down, scrutinizing him through the windshield as if her life depended on her estimate of him.

She saw full into an engaging face, the blue eyes gazing at her with something winning and yet amused in them. It gave her the strangest shock, too. For an instant it was almost as if she were seeing Dale again. Her mind reeled. The boy on the highway had now seen she was alone. He even stepped back. He didn't expect a girl, driving alone, to pick him up. His stepping back tipped the scales in his favor. He was no road cat who might prove dangerous.

She stopped, leaning to the right to speak to him through the window. His eyes were very blue, surprised at the great luck of having her stop. He waited for her to speak first. He was watching her, though, with a sort of masculine effrontery which was appealing. In that fleeting instant before she spoke she was reminded that her own eyes were also blue, almost as blue as his. Years ago, sometimes strangers had assumed Dale and she were brother and sister. Oh, God! This boy on the road was so much like Dale. A bored copper glancing in at the two of them also might think they were related. It was a chance!

"Hello," she said pleasantly, at a cost to her nerves he would never guess from the smooth lovely face turned to him. "Can I give you a lift?"

Chapter Three

Bill Evans was surprised to have the Plymouth stop. He had come quite a distance this morning. He had so much farther to go, so very many miles, that he wouldn't have much liked knowing that that pretty blonde girl in the Plymouth had stopped because she was frightened and desperate and prepared to use him anyway she could to save herself.

Bill Evans had started off about seven this morning. Right away he had better luck than he had anticipated. Four miles west of his uncle's farm an empty truck had stopped for him. When the driver asked, "How far?" Bill answered, "Dexter," which was only the next town. They arrived at Dexter in a quarter of an hour. The driver said, "Here it is. I go to Stuart. How far you really going?"

"I'd settle for Stuart," Bill admitted.

The truck driver started up again. "You haven't done much hitchhiking?"

"Not too much."

"It's this way. Don't bother with women driving alone or a fellow and his girl. They won't stop. Salesmen going through—sometimes they'll stop. Guys like me in their own trucks, they'll stop. The big transcontinental trucks won't. Don't say you're going too far because people might not want to get stuck with a long haul. But don't go chicken, either. Next time, if somebody stops to pick you up give yourself a chance at a fifty- or hundred-mile ride. If they ain't going that far, they'll say so."

So Bill got into Stuart by eight-thirty in the morning and continued on shank's mare. He had never felt so free in his life. He had twenty-two dollars. He could eat on a dollar a day or less—a dollar would still get you a loaf of bread, a bottle of milk, cheese, or peanut butter, and maybe a chocolate bar to carry you through the lunch hour.

If he did a hundred miles every day he'd be in Sacramento within twenty days, with ten dollars left for emergencies. If he started falling short of a hundred miles a day, after the first week he'd have to hunt a job until he'd earned enough to hit the road again. It was that simple.

Nobody picked him up. Cars passed him, wham, wham, like that. But it was still all right. He had prepared himself not to expect very much. He wasn't a road cat or a phony college boy with a sign on the coy side or someone too lazy or too soft to keep plugging the miles on his own legs. He had his bag on his shoulder and his hands in his pockets and all at once he found he was whistling, "California, Here I Come." It was an old tune with a lilt that lifted you. Unexpectedly he remembered his father used to whistle it.

A big brindle-colored bulldog squeezed from under a wire fence, growling at Bill. He knew enough to stop, sticking out his hand, palm down. The dog smelled his fingers while Bill spoke gently.

So Bill walked along, the dog trundling behind. It was a fine morning. Bill forgot to stop and thumb when he heard a car coming. It shot by. Baggage was piled everywhere, roped on top, with a New York license showing. Probably that car was rolling straight through to the west coast. Bill took a long breath. Perhaps a car like that might stop for him, with somebody saying, "Get in."

The dog was still following him. He stopped and told it to go home, and somewhere to his left a girl's voice unexpectedly called, "Say, that's my dog. Butch! Here, Butch!"

She was standing halfway up an orchard stepladder, filling a basket with early ripening June cherries. He saw her sandals, socks thicker than his and a bright red, sturdy bare legs, the jeans rolled above her knees, the checkered shirt. Instead of being protected with a hat or scarf, her hair fell thick and tangled to her shoulders, black as pitch.

As he saw her, suddenly it seemed he was years older. Once, not so long ago, he might have thought she was sensational or almost sensational. But he had passed through that stage. He was finished with it. If she'd been a little older she would have known how to wipe off the blurred edges of lipstick and have cut her hair or kept it neat and protected from the leaves and twigs.

Bill said easily, "I used to have a dog like that."

The bulldog crawled under the lowest wire of the fence, wagging its tail regretfully at Bill. The girl looked at Bill. Whatever she saw about him must have reassured her for she stepped down from the ladder, and they talked back and forth over the fence for a few minutes. It was a swell morning, wasn't it? She'd decided to make herself a cherry pie. Imagine. She had to learn sometime. It was talk like that, not important, but just nice to be talking a minute or so.

She tossed back the hair over her shoulders. It was the kind of hair you'd like to dip your hands in. Probably she knew, too, her shirt shouldn't be unbuttoned quite so low, but it did show nice brown curves. From his height of six feet he looked down upon her and decided lazily that for her own good someone ought to spank her. Why was it so many younger girls felt they had to prove every minute they were sensational?

"How far you going?" she finally asked.

He didn't see why he couldn't tell her. "California."

"A boy has all the luck. If my grades are good enough, Dad's promised I can enter Drake next year. But where's that for going anywhere? Only

Des Moines." She sighed. "Here. Hold out your hands."

She started to pour cherries into his hands but had a better idea. Her jacket was folded across the crossbar holding the ladder legs. She pulled out the rolled newspaper from her jacket pocket, tore off half a sheet, rolled it into a big funnel and dumped in half her cherries.

"There."

He thanked her and said he bet her pie turned out fine. The cherries were delicious, tartly sweet. At the end of the fence he turned and waved to her and she waved back.

For a time no cars or trucks went by, going west, at all. He finished the cherries. The half-torn newspaper page was the comic section of the same paper his aunt and uncle subscribed to. For lack of something else to do, he unrolled it to see what had happened to his three favorites this morning. Unfortunately, the page had been torn diagonally from the upper left corner to the right. The top strip, Mr. Future, had its full complement of panels, but his three favorites had no ending panels.

He glanced at Mr. Future and saw the beautiful girl was still doing something in the time machine and he threw away the scrap of paper. He had once eagerly followed this strip until either he had outgrown it or it had become so impossible it stuck in his craw.

When he was younger Bill had uneasily wondered why somebody in charge of the newspaper syndicate hadn't cautioned the artist to make her clothing less gossamer. Possibly it was because drawing the girl like that had increased circulation.

As he walked along he found himself wondering if the artist who drew Mr. Future had a model whom he used for drawing Fancy McMerry, as the girl in the strip was so charmingly called. Then he realized where his thoughts were drifting under this bright June-morning sun; he laughed at himself and increased his stride.

He thought all his first luck of the morning must have changed the sequence, or something, for anything else following through.

Finally, about nine-thirty, he did receive another push forward on wheels. A red delivery Dodge stopped, a sign on its panels saying: "Old Farm Brand Coffee & Spices." The man inside could have been thirty-five to fifty. He had one of those leathery, Irish-looking faces, with a nose which once must have stopped a fist, and his voice was a growl.

"Get in. Get in."

When they were on their way Bill was asked the inevitable question, but this time he didn't cut the distance too short. He answered, "Council Bluffs". The man who said his name was Ed Murvon grunted that he was going as far as Casey. That was only about ten miles, but every lift Bill got jumped him that much faster. Bill was grateful. Ed Murvon began to warm up a trifle. He was like that brindle bulldog back there, growling at first on general principles. He had Bill hold the wheel while he packed shag tobacco into an old brier pipe, blackened and worn.

When Ed took the wheel, puffing at his pipe, he cast another glance at Bill. "Isn't that an old Ninth Air Force insignia on your sleeve? You don't go back that far, do you, son?"

"No, it was my father's."

"Was it? I used to be in that outfit. What did you say your name was?"

Bill hadn't said. He hadn't planned to give his real name to anyone giving him a lift, at least until he was far enough away to feel safe. The chance that Ed Murvon might have known his father, however, made Bill forget.

"Bill Evans. My father was William Evans—Major Evans. You didn't—"

"Major Evans?" Ed shook his head. "Nope. I guess not."

"He was shot down in Forty-three."

"One of those ball-bearing raids?"

"That's what we heard."

"I'm sorry," Ed said, sounding as if he meant it. "I was only with the outfit a few months early in Forty-four. I got transferred."

All at once Ed started talking about something else, how tough it was getting to brace farm wives day after day. This was going to be his last summer in the business. His wife had inherited a pear orchard out in Oregon. Next fall, the two of them were moving to Oregon. Then he asked where Bill was from. And Bill didn't know whether to tell the truth or play it safe.

He didn't have to decide because suddenly a narrow concrete bridge rushed at them. A big truck was booming down at them, beyond the bridge. It looked as if the big truck would pass over the bridge at the same time and maybe squeeze the light delivery. Right then, something happened that Bill hadn't anticipated. Ed Murvon stepped on the gas; the red delivery truck jumped like a thunderbolt. It must have accelerated from thirty-five miles an hour to sixty in those three seconds, tearing past bridge and big truck, the needle swinging up to seventy and still moving until Ed took his foot from the throttle.

Bill said, "Have you got a souped-up engine under that hood, Mr. Murvon?"

"Why, no, just an ordinary old Dodge engine," said Ed casually, perhaps too casually Bill decided when he thought about it later. "I guess it was enough downgrade for us to pick up some speed."

Bill didn't remember it was downgrade. But he didn't say anything because Ed had entered the town, drawing up in front of the municipal building. That was the trouble with this lousy business of peddling coffee and spices, Ed growled. The local merchants in nearly every town had passed ordinances requiring you to get a license unless you wanted to be soaked with a fine. Bill got out on the sidewalk, waiting for Ed to come around the other side so he could thank him.

"I tell you what, son. I might finish my business in half an hour or so. If I do I could take you as far as Atlantic but I can't tell. I might get stuck the rest of the day. Wait if you want."

Bill hesitated. The sun was getting warmer. It seemed to him he hadn't put enough distance behind him yet, to risk hanging around on the possible chance of being carried closer to Council Bluffs. Ed said, "Here's what. If someone doesn't pick you up during the next half hour or so keep an eye peeled for my red delivery truck."

"Thanks, I will."

As Bill stepped behind the truck he noticed the two rear doors had swung open. They must have jarred open when crossing that bridge. If Ed Murvon wasn't careful he'd lose everything inside the truck. He said, "Mr. Murvon, your doors are open," and started to close them—and stopped, for there was no sign at all of shelves or racks or cans of coffee and spices inside the compartment. It was nearly empty. All Bill saw was an old bedroll tossed on one side as if Ed Murvon liked to camp by the side of the road. Hanging from a stanchion above the bedroll was something that looked like a forty-five stuck into a shabby holster. But Bill didn't have much of a chance to see anything very distinctly. A hard shoulder shoved against him, almost pushing him off balance. Ed Murvon slammed the doors shut. He turned, the crooked black pipe still gripped between the big even teeth. Under the shaggy red eyebrows the eyes were like small pebbles. But he was smiling broadly.

"I'm supposed to get my consignment of spices and coffee at the depot," Ed told Bill. "That's another thing about this lousy racket of mine. If you have a good week of selling, hell, you're liable to have to wait around a couple of days for the home office in Des Moines to send you a new consignment. Well, look for me in half an hour or so if I don't get stuck here."

"Sure," Bill said. "Thanks, Mr. Murvon."

He began walking toward the highway, trying not to walk too fast. It wasn't necessary to glance over his shoulder at the red delivery truck. He'd noticed the rear plate. It was an Illinois license plate. Maybe the home office was in Des Moines as Mr. Murvon had said; but Mr. Murvon's red delivery truck, with nothing inside it but a bedroll and a forty-five revolver, had Illinois numbers.

Bill began walking. For a time he had a jumpy feeling, thinking it might be that red delivery truck whenever a car suddenly spilled its wham of sound while passing from behind him. If he sighted that red delivery truck coming toward him he had decided to slip off the road and up into one of the fields of new corn. After thirty minutes passed, by the watch which had once been his father's, he began to feel less uneasy.

At eleven o'clock Bill decided he had walked six miles in the past hour. He was beginning to be hungry. He would have to learn to tighten his belt and keep going past grocery stores and restaurants during the noon hour to keep within a dollar a day. He couldn't afford more than breakfast and something at night.

Ahead of him the road slid downgrade through a stand of pines and turned right, disappearing behind the pines to appear a mile or so beyond, where it climbed over a green rolling of farm land.

A Ford slugged by, going west. It was followed by a Cadillac in a hurry, as usual. After that came a long interval when there was no traffic on the road.

He passed another mile sign. He was 3.4 miles from Adair and 25.6 miles from Atlantic.

The summer breeze sighing through the pines carried the fresh moistness of showers. Next, he heard the hollow sound of another car coming downgrade, echoing back and forth between the trees. He stepped off the road, wanting a lift very much before real rain started falling.

It was a blue Plymouth coupe. As it approached he saw a girl was driving. Well, that was no good. It was too much to hope that a girl would stop. He stepped back, off the highway. However, to his surprise the Plymouth slowed down and stopped. The very pretty blonde girl looked him over a moment or so, smiled pleasantly, and said, "Hello. Can I give you a lift?"

"Thank you very much," Bill said.

She opened the door for him. To make room for him she picked up her camel's-hair coat and threw it carelessly on the shelf behind her, covering a shabby leather bag next to a new canvas suitcase with a Drake U sticker on it. Bill thought she looked like a college girl. Probably she was driving home for the summer from Drake University in Des Moines. As he got in he saw a flash of bright color on the seat and reached down and picked up a hand-painted man's silk tie.

The girl started driving again, slipping in the clutch jerkily. Bill rocked forward and back. She was a hell of a driver, he thought, amused. She was a good looker, though. She was so pretty she nearly took your breath away. It was hard not to stare at her while she was busy shifting and getting the Plymouth under way.

While she was dressed casually for traveling in a yellow pull-over, pleated skirt, tan nylons, and tan leather loafers, Bill knew enough about girl's clothes to know that casual effect hadn't been obtained through any mailorder catalogue. Her corn-silk-colored hair was pulled smoothly from her forehead and tied in a thick double loop at the nape of her neck. Her lips had a soft pink coloring, without the brightness of lipstick. She looked pale and there were bluish shadows around her blue eyes. He wondered if maybe she had been on a graduation party last night and hadn't had much sleep.

She said, "Where you going?"

"Council Bluffs."

"When you're driving alone I guess it's not so hot to pick up somebody for a lift," she said, smiling a little, giving him a quick glance. "But you didn't look very risky. It's not much fun walking, is it? I'm Alma Lathrop, by the way."

"I'm Bill Evans. I'm obliged for the lift. Say, I found this tie on the seat. I didn't want to sit on it and get it dirty."

He felt the car twist erratically as if it had passed over a hump in the road. Next, it steadied itself. Alma Lathrop's eyes flicked toward him again, seeing the tie he was holding in his hand.

"My heavens, I didn't know it was there. I bought it last week for my brother-in-law's birthday and decided not to give it to him at the last minute because it was sorta gaudy. Where'd you find it?"

"On the seat," he repeated.

"It must have got stuffed behind the seat cushion. Throw it away. I don't want it."

He looked at the tie. The silk was rich and heavy. It was a genuine hand-painted tie, all right. While perhaps it was a little gaudy, he didn't like throwing it away. The knitted label inside the lining was lettered, "Crabtree's, Ltd., Omaha." You didn't find knitted labels on cheap ties. It must have cost her ten or twelve dollars.

"Throw it away?" he asked.

Something in his voice made her say carelessly, "Keep it, if you like."

"I couldn't do that, Miss Lathrop."

"Nonsense. If you don't want it, throw it away."

"Well, I'll keep it then. Thank you."

She didn't even answer. When he looked at her, she seemed to be even more pale. She was driving over the white line and back to one side again. She removed her right hand from the wheel, pressing it to her forehead.

"I've got an awful headache, Bill. My grandmother's supposed to meet me in Atlantic. I don't suppose you'd—"

"I'd be glad to," Bill said quickly.

For a minute or so he had been afraid she might pass out. Sometimes his aunt had had those blinding headaches. Once, she had nearly wrecked his uncle's old Buick.

They stopped and changed places and Alma said gratefully, "Gosh, I hate driving anyway."

"It's good to get behind a wheel again."

They passed through a small town and the road sign at the end of town said Atlantic was 21 miles. Bill wished it would be longer than that. Alma had curled up in the seat, making herself comfortable. Even if she did have that drawn taut look she was still the prettiest girl he ever had seen.

He said, "I guess you're from Drake?"

"How did you know?"

"I saw that sticker on your suitcase."

"I graduated two days ago. Where are you from, Bill?"

"Well, my uncle's farm was outside Adel. I was living with them."

She smiled. "Now you're on your way to see your parents?"

"Well, no. They aren't alive."

"Oh."

"Father got his in the war. Mother died five years ago."

"That's tough. Have you got a job in Council Bluffs?"

"Not exactly—" He hesitated. He didn't like lying to her. "The truth is, I just said Council Bluffs because you asked me, Miss Lathrop. When you're hitching rides, sometimes if you say how far you really—"

"My God!" The friendly quality had drained from her voice. "You aren't running away from something, are you? If you're in trouble—"

"I'm not in trouble."

"Guy, slow down, will you? What's your pitch? Give it to me quick."

He drove at thirty miles an hour while he gave it to her as quickly as he could. After the war his mother had held a secretarial job on a Sacramento newspaper until the morning she had been late to work, had run for the bus, and had fallen in front of the bus instead of ever catching it. Bill believed the editor of the newspaper might still remember him even if it was five years ago when Bill had been sent back to an aunt, his mother's older sister, and her husband in Iowa. He hoped for a part-time job. He planned to work his way through the first year at Sacramento College, complete his military service, finish college when he returned, and eventually become the kind of newspaperman his father had been.

"Gosh." The friendly quality was running through her voice again. "It's a long hike to California. I've got a sister out there. It's a nice place to live, but I'd hate having to hike that distance. Wouldn't your uncle give you money for a train or bus?"

"Uncle Otis and I didn't get along too well."

All the time she was speaking to him she was watching the road through the windshield, as if she was still not too certain of his driving ability. He was trying to drive very carefully. Her headache must be fierce. Her lips were nearly bloodless.

"Does your uncle know you've gone?"

"Not yet. He and Aunt Daisy are in Des Moines for a couple of days. He won't try to get me back, though. He used up my father's insurance money when he wasn't supposed to touch it. He'll be pleased to be rid of me."

"All your money?"

"All but twenty-two dollars I earned giving tennis lessons on Saturdays."

"You ought to have him jailed."

"No. All I want is never to see him again."

"Bill, how old are you?"

He hesitated. He wanted very much to say he was older than he was. But she had been straightforward and trusting with him. "Eighteen," he answered.

"My gracious. I thought you were at least twenty. With those big shoulders of yours I'll bet you played football."

"Well, yes, I did."

He wondered why girls a few years older than you were seemed to enjoy flustering you by making such personal remarks. It was as if they knew and you knew there was an invisible barrier erected between the two of you and it amused them to look across the barrier at you. If she'd been that black-haired girl back there on the road who'd given him the ripe cherries and had been so very young and tried so very hard to be sensational, probably he would have casually answered he'd placed last fall on the all-state high-school team selection. The young black-haired girl would have been impressed. He'd have been the one immeasurably older and more experienced. He doubted if Alma would be very impressed.

He had to keep his eyes mostly on the road and he only heard her voice, light and friendly, saying,

"I'm twenty-two. Twenty-two probably makes me an awfully old hag to you, doesn't it? Gosh! Imagine being eighteen again. You can have it, honey."

He was beginning to enjoy driving with her and wished it didn't have to end so quickly. They were about halfway to Atlantic. The shower had ended. The sky was a bright June blue and the sun was shining all over the rolling farm country and the air had a fresh brightness, and Bill glanced toward Alma and back to the road and all of a sudden wanted to tell her he'd never seen any girl in his life as pretty as she was. But it would be nervy, maybe, for him to say it, when he'd known her less than thirty minutes. He was lucky to get the chance to be driving a Plymouth as far as Atlantic.

"Twenty-two isn't very old," he said, trying to sound casual.

"Girls start off being twice as old as boys," she said, smiling a little. "My gracious. You're just a child, still."

Even if she was teasing him, it nettled him slightly. "I used to play tennis with a girl in our town. Thelma Binns. She was runner-up in the Midwestern singles a year ago. She's twenty-five but when she felt like it she could kid around as much as a high-school girl."

She gave him an odd cool glance. "Did she kid around with you, honey? All girls one time or another like to have a play with a younger boy. Did you find that out, yet?"

He was even more nettled. He didn't know how he'd happened to think of Thelma. He shouldn't have mentioned her name. He'd been bragging a little, he supposed. It served him right, trying to act older than he was. An older girl had more to her than high-school kids. Usually she had too much to her. She could coast over you any time she felt like it. You'd be doing fine, then all of a sudden you'd have a helpless frustrated feeling, when one of them would say something you didn't quite know how to answer. He remembered Thelma had the same amused frank way, asking him questions a younger girl never would have asked, and laughing when she had embarrassed him. It made you think she was, somehow, getting back at you against men of her own age and older.

He said steadily, "Miss Binns went to Iowa State. She was written up last year in the papers when she married a Chicago banker. Perhaps you know her, Miss Lathrop?"

"No, I haven't heard of her, honey," Alma said carelessly. "Now, Bill, let's don't be so formal. Can that 'Miss Lathrop' routine, will you? Just—Oh, God! Look!"

Her voice sounded as if she was going to be sick.

As they came around another turn, a quarter of a mile ahead of them Bill saw two automobiles were stopped while men from a third car were asking questions. Now the first of the two automobiles moved away. A tall man was peering in a window of the second car. Bill heard Alma suck in her breath.

"Bill, what'll I do?" she asked. "They're probably after me. I—I was speeding in that town just before I gave you a lift. I—ran away from the motorcycle cop."

"It's a traffic count or something, Miss Lathrop. They wouldn't be after you."

"They are. I'm sure they are." She cast him an urgent appealing glance. "Oh, Bill, if I'm arrested I won't know how to explain to Granny. Your hair and eyes are almost the color of mine. Could you say I'm your sister—anything—you've been with me—and I'm not—"

Her voice choked. She was terrified. He felt instant sympathy for her. "Sure," Bill said. "Don't worry."

The second car drove away and one of the men from the third car stepped into the highway. The man raised his hand in a signal for Bill to slow down. He was wearing a slouch hat, military-style shirt with a star on it, a service gun on his hip, whipcords, and dusty boots. The two other deputy sheriffs waited in the parked car.

Alma whispered, "Please, Bill. I'll pay you. Anything—"

He said, "It's all right."

He stopped and stuck his head through the window. Suddenly everything became very ordinary. It was nothing to be alarmed about; he recognized the man with the sheriff's badge. It was Mr. Bradley, one of the referees in most of the games Bill's team had played last fall. Mr. Bradley was a tall angular man who could get over the field as fast as a big elk, and he tried always to be absolutely fair.

Bill said, "Hello, Mr. Bradley. I thought you were sheriff of Clearfield County when you weren't refereeing football games. What are you doing this far south?"

Mr. Bradley stepped to the car and bent down. He looked at Bill for a second or so and said, "Say, I do know you, don't I?" He squinted slightly, smiling. "Why, sure I do. Never forgit a face."

"I knew you right away."

"That was a good run you made Thanksgiving. Yes, sir, I hated having to call the play over because that feller was off side." He peered across Bill at Alma and said apologetically, "Howdy, Miss."

"My sister's scared you flagged us down because I was speeding. If I was speeding, I didn't know it."

"Why, no. Nothing like that. No, we blocked off most of the roads down here because—" Mr. Bradley stepped back, and his voice grew more kindly. "This is only a sort of road check, you might say. We don't mean to cause young people like you and your sister no trouble."

He pulled a sticker from a pad, wet it with his tongue, pasted it to the left-hand corner of the windshield, scribbled a date, time, and his signature on it. Then he stood back and said, "There now, that shows I've passed you through. Nobody'll give you any more trouble. That was a fine game you played last Thanksgiving, yes, sir. So long, young fellow."

Chapter Four

Alma filled her cramped lungs as Bill drove the Plymouth away. She had done it! She had passed through. It kept coming and coming to her. Bill had been really magnificent in an emergency. Why, with that sticker she could drive clear across Iowa into Nebraska! She smiled gratefully at him.

"Bill, what luck! You must be quite a football player."

"Not much. He'd even forgotten my name from last fall."

That was all the better. Now no one could ever trace her by knowing it was Bill Evans driving the blue Plymouth. She was so pleased with herself for sighting Bill along the road and leaping at the chance given her that for a minute or so she felt the blood pounding back through her veins.

But her momentary relief was spoiled by the need to think ahead. In ten or fifteen more minutes they'd be in Atlantic. There Bill would get out, leave her, and once more she would be by herself, having to go on to that dreadful little grocery store.

It was nearly one o'clock. It was impossible to know what had happened, but she didn't dare switch on the radio for another news broadcast. She might give herself completely away in front of Bill, although he was saying cheerfully enough:

"You mustn't let small-town policemen worry you, Miss Lathrop. I'd rather deal with one of them than a big-city cop. Though, I suppose it's different for you, if you live in Des Moines and are used to city police."

"I don't live there," she said, trying to keep her voice even. The mounting terror again was pricking at her. "I went to college there, that's all."

He probably was curious about where she lived. But he was too polite to ask. He was terribly nice. How different than Monk! She felt a wave of disgust, hating Monk. Evert if Bill had dust on his jacket and pants he looked clean. He even smelled clean. It was difficult to believe he was only eighteen. He must be well over six feet, but he was as thin as a rail, like a young hickory tree. That uncle of his probably hadn't fed him very well. Suddenly, surprised at herself for thinking about Bill, she wished with all her heart that he got quickly to California. She wanted to do something for him. She had saved over two thousand dollars of her own money. She wondered if he would accept twenty dollars when they got to Atlantic.

Leave her! Her heart cried out in panic. She could see herself in a few more minutes having to walk into strange grocery store to look for some huge flaccid old creature whom she had only once seen, and then only briefly. Suppose police were waiting for her and Monk instead of Gramma? They would grab her with all the hot money she was carrying in the Plymouth. By now, Monk might have been found, shot perhaps, or taken away to Boone.

Bill had been wonderful in that other emergency. Her mind revolted against the next insidious thought. It would be mean of her to persuade him to go into that store. He had been too decent. But how would it be any risk for Bill? She could say her grandmother was supposed to be waiting for her in the store. Instead of describing Gramma to Bill, a huge gray-faced man, she would describe a little old white-haired lady. Bill just wouldn't find any little old white-haired lady in the store.

All right! Bill could safely enter the store. He wouldn't see the little old lady in the smartly tailored suit; he'd return and say she wasn't there. Alma could ask who had been in the store. It would be that simple.

She would get rid of him, then. Twenty dollars was probably too much to give him; he'd wonder about that. Five dollars? She wanted to give him more. He was brown as a berry. Think of going all the way to California! She wished she was going. She didn't know what would happen to her after she stepped into the store. God, how she wished she had never got in such a mess. Monk had never told her what would happen, either, after she contacted

Gramma. It was like being carried toward a great gulf. She felt her legs tremble.

Bill said, "We're about there. Another mile. I can't tell you how much obliged I am to you for the lift, Miss Lathrop. That tie's a beauty, too. Sure you don't want it?"

"Gracious, no. I don't know why I bought it." She had to do it right. He couldn't become suspicious of her. "If it's not too much trouble, Bill, would you do me a big favor?"

"Yes, sure," he said promptly.

She caught a glimpse of herself in the rear-view mirror. She did look like hell, her eyes staring half out of her head. All the better. She let herself slump in the seat. She was no good. How easy it was for her to lie when she was in trouble!

"Bill, I just feel lousy. I guess it's something I ate last night. Granny's promised to wait for me at a blue and red grocery store, near the railroad station. She's smaller than I am, white haired, and she'll be wearing a checked tailored suit. If she's there, you can't miss her. She might not have waited for me, though. I probably look like a hag and I hate going into a strange grocery store. Would you mind going in for me? It'll only take you a minute."

"No, of course not," Bill said. "Be glad to."

He didn't mind at all going into the store to look for her grandmother, although he wished he was better dressed and not quite so dusty looking. Those headaches, he knew, could be fierce. He felt sorry for Miss Lathrop. He snatched another look at her. But he saw only her slim shoulder and the smooth hair, pulled back to the thick knot at the nape of her neck. She was staring out of the window on her side as if he didn't exist any more. She was close enough for him to reach out and touch her arm, and it surprised him that momentarily he felt an urge to put an arm around the neat lovely shoulders, even if she was four years older than he was, and say, "Just rest your head on my shoulder, shut your eyes, and take it easy. Sometimes those damned headaches go away as quickly as they come."

He didn't, of course. Nevertheless, just driving along with her toward Atlantic, smelling the fresh warm scent of her yellow hair, started him thinking about picking up her grandmother and wondering if, afterward, they might even allow him to go along all the way to Council Bluffs. He was tempted to ask but decided against it. If Miss Lathrop had wanted him to go all the way she would have mentioned it. She had given him this much of a lift. He had no right to press her, particularly when she was feeling so miserable.

Still, it gave him an excited feeling to think of continuing farther with her. It was something like the feeling he used to have just before the kickoff of an important game. It was not quite that, though, because there was something else in it, too. He knew what it was but he didn't like to admit it to himself.

Without meaning to, his mind went back to that day last summer when he'd been helping Thelma Binns with her backhand stroke. While he wasn't anything particular at tennis he did have a powerful serve. Thelma must have been about twenty-four, engaged to a Chicago man, and the daughter of the town's richest grain dealer. She had believed Bill might go somewhere in tennis if he want to put in the time, and she had even been willing to arrange to have him coached by the local pro. But Bill had never had the time. His uncle wouldn't have given him the time, anyway.

Each Saturday afternoon, Thelma had paid Bill five dollars to bat balls at her as hard as he could. That last Saturday, last summer, she had driven him from the country club to his uncle's farm. Next day she was leaving for Chicago. They were both hot and pleasantly fatigued, an after a quick shower at the club she had changed into crisp white shorts and a jersey sweater, wrapping a towel around her neck. Thelma was a big girl, a big strapping girl, and she drove her own red Chrysler.

On the way to the farm she started teasing Bill about the little curly haired girl who'd been playing a very bad game of singles in the court opposite them. The little curly haired girl had not lived in town very long and Bill knew she was only in her second or third year of high school. But Thelma was saying the girl had a big crush on Bill. Anyone could see it. Bill had really been very mean to little Clara.

It annoyed Bill unreasonably to have Thelma tease him like that. Finally, because he trusted Thelma, and possibly needed someone to confide in, he had tried to tell her about his uncle. In the time he had lived with his aunt and uncle, to his chagrin and humiliation Bill had learned what invariably happened if he had many dates with any of the girls whom he liked and who had appeared to like him.

"I tell you, Thelma," he had said angrily, "it's no use. Clara hasn't lived here long enough to learn about my uncle. If I take her to a movie or a dance, he'll hear about it. The town's too small. Sooner or later he'll have a chance to see her mother or father and he'll start asking questions. Does Clara go to church? Is she a nice girl? I don't think he knows how he sounds. It's no use trying to argue with him. He doesn't even understand. He's kind of crazy on the subject. But it's embarrassing. It makes a fool out of me. It's—" He groped for words. "It's no use," he had ended, rather helplessly. "I've finally learned it causes less trouble all around simply not to have dates."

But Thelma had said tolerantly, "Oh, go on, Bill. You're imagining it. Perhaps your uncle's a little peculiar, but he sees my father in business, doesn't he? He's never made any cracks against me to my father—and you and I've been seeing each other every Saturday, haven't we?"

She didn't understand. Bill tried to tell her. Perhaps that was the mistake. Last summer she was twenty-four, at least seven years older than he had been. His uncle wouldn't ever have thought of including Thelma among those younger girls of Bill's age whom he considered the real danger. Thelma had listened, not answering; but instead of continuing on the main road she had unexpectedly turned off on one of the shady side roads. An expression that Bill had never quite understood came over her blunt but rather handsome face.

"Bill, your uncle's an old fool, if you want to know," she had said huskily, stopping the car. Afterward, nothing much had really happened. It was simply that he still remembered the sharpness of the excitement which was not at all like the excitement of the kickoff before a big game. Thelma had turned. He didn't quite know how she came into his arms. She was kissing him as eagerly as he found he was kissing her. They were still warm from playing tennis and of a sudden he could smell her woman's smell and his own smell, somehow mingling; and the excitement was like a pain.

"Don't, Bill," she had said, all at once shoving herself free. "This won't get either of us anywhere. You'd better get out and walk. It's not too far. I still say you ought to do something about your tennis."

He had never done anything about his tennis because he had never had the time or the money. But he still remembered how it had been that Saturday afternoon, last summer, with Thelma. Unexpectedly, for no reason understood, the same painful strain of excitement was carrying him now, here in the Plymouth with Alma. He was ashamed. She wasn't big and strapping and capable of taking care of herself as Thelma Binns had been.

She was very small, neat, fresh, and lovely, silently worried, with the thick yellow hair skinned back from the rounded beauty of her forehead as if she was trying her best to look plain as possible, instead of being someone who could catch at your heart if she wished.

After entering the town of Atlantic he drove along the street parallel to the railroad track, following Alma's directions. A freight car was on the siding. Two big grain elevators towered above green elms shading the street. At the end of the long block was a shabby grocery store, painted blue and red.

Alma said, "Bill, park here, will you please? Let me wait for you here in the shade. It's so hot. I expected to be here by noon. Granny's probably given me up and taken the bus to Council Bluffs,"

He opened the door on his side, aware of how dusty and disheveled he must look. He felt self-conscious about going into a store to seek out a small elderly woman whom he'd never seen. But Miss Lathrop did look terribly pale. She worried him. She shouldn't be driving a car on a hot day like this. Again, he thought of suggesting he was willing, very willing indeed, to chauffeur her and her grandmother to Council Bluffs. But she hadn't suggested it. It would look as if he was pushing himself too hard. Maybe she expected her grandmother to do the driving.

"I forgot to ask you her name."

Alma lifted her head. "Her name? Mrs. Ralph Lathrop. Hurry, Bill."

"I'd better brush myself off."

"You look all right," she said impatiently.

He got out of the car. "I don't want your grandmother to think you picked up a bum," he said. Miss Lathrop looked as if she had plenty of money, and her grandmother would probably be one of these distinguished old city ladies with that blue color in her white hair. He felt for the tie in his pocket. That might help. He didn't want to look too much like a roughneck.

"Please, hurry," Alma said.

He walked under the shady elms, tying his tie, and trying to straighten the old windbreaker. If he had any luck in Sacramento and got that newspaper job, in a month or so he could look forward to buying a decent suit and all the fixings. His uncle shouldn't have taken that insurance money! There was no use thinking about it now, though. It was ended. It was all fading into the past. He'd earn his own money. And he had had luck today. What was he beefing about? Here he was in Atlantic, four times as far as he'd expected to be this morning.

As he turned to enter the store he brushed against a thin girl whose lemon-colored hair looked as if she'd been experimenting with one of those new coloring powders for women's hair. She stopped so abruptly her hair even shook off a faint dusty metallic cloud.

"Sorry—"

"My fault," she said. "I'm always in too much of a hurry."

He stepped back to let her enter first and walked through the door after her. When he tried to study it out later, to piece it together, it always seemed to him that walking into the store had been the turning point.

In the store there was no elderly little woman. He saw only a wispy man behind the meat counter, chopping meat. A second man in a bright-blue suit was looking at packaged seeds. No one else was in here except the lemon-haired girl who had just entered and himself. He stopped, deciding to return to Alma. The girl with the lemon colored hair was in front of him, going toward the meat counter.

Immediately, everything began splintering. The man in the bright-blue suit stepped over to Bill, grabbed hold of his tie and pulled Bill forward. "So you're the punk," he snarled, let go the tie, stepped back, and whipped out an automatic from a shoulder holster. Bill had a moment of stupefaction. The girl with the lemon-colored hair gave a yelp.

The man in the blue suit swerved half around to her saying viciously, "You want it first, blondy?"

The fool actually was going to shoot her. On reflex, more than anything, Bill swung his right. Everything happened in split seconds. Something bright flashed in the dim air. There was a heavy clunk. The man in the blue suit toppled forward, and Bill's fist never did connect. The grocery man had leaned over the counter, striking hard with the flat side of a meat cleaver. Stunned, Bill looked down at the unconscious fool in the bright-blue suit. Horrified he was thinking of what might have been the result if the grocer had struck with the sharp edge of the cleaver.

"Erma," the grocer shouted furiously, "what trouble you in now?"

"Poppa, I don't know what you're talking about!"

They were ignoring Bill. He kicked the automatic across the floor, several yards away from the nerveless claw of hand.

"Painting your face! Dyeing your hair! Oh, a daughter like you I should have. Now you got a fella who should want to kill you!"

"Poppa, I don't know either of these fellas!"

"You—" The grocer shook the meat cleaver at Bill. "You should be ashamed of yourself. Getting my daughter in such trouble so another fella waits here to shoot her, yet! Get out of here."

Chapter Five

Alma listened to Bill's half-concerned, half-amused explanation and it made no sense to her, at all. She had a frozen sensation, listening. What had gone wrong? Bill was saying no one had been in that store except the screwball who'd tried to shoot a girl; a girl, a storekeeper, and Bill, himself. Where was Gramma? Something must have gone wrong. Here she was, left way out on a limb.

Without thinking, she said sharply, "Get in. Don't just stand there."

Bill's expression had changed. She'd better get hold of herself, she thought. Where was Gramma? Why hadn't Gramma been waiting? It was incomprehensible. Bill was in the car, looking at her. What did he want? She hadn't even told him where to drive. Her head was swimming. Bill mustn't see how scared she was. If the coppers got her they'd lock her up for years. She might even burn.

She leaned forward, trying desperately to smile. "Don't you want to drive me to Council Bluffs, Bill?"

He had jumped at it, like a big friendly puppy being offered a bone. You could almost see his tail wagging, she thought, he was so pleased to continue on with her. She felt the car carrying her out of town. Now they were on the highway again. Oh, God, what was there for her in Council Bluffs? She had said Council Bluffs to Bill because she had to keep pretending she had a dear old granny waiting for her. What was she to do?

She asked, "You're certain Granny wasn't there, Bill?"

"I looked for her. Nobody was there, except that screwball in the blue suit, the girl, the grocer, and me. That was all."

That was all. It was terrifying. She couldn't understand it. She saw he was worried about her, evidently assuming she had counted on meeting her grandmother.

He even asked, "Shouldn't we stop and telephone to Council Bluffs to see if your grandmother's there?"

"That won't be necessary," she said quickly. "Granny—must have gone on ahead. She'll be waiting for me in Council Bluffs."

What had happened? She was at a dead end. Where was Gramma? Then Alma thought of all that money just behind her head, crammed inside the leather bag. A hundred thousand dollars! Monk had never told her who Gramma was or where Gramma's headquarters was located.

It dawned on her suddenly. *She* had that hundred thousand dollars! That sticker on the windshield would carry her safely through any road blocks as far as Council Bluffs. If she could only get away! What would Monk do? Monk was left far behind. It hadn't been her fault that Gramma hadn't been waiting at the pickup station. It wouldn't be her fault if Monk got picked up today or tomorrow by the sheriffs or coppers. Her heart felt bruised. She gripped her hands together—and became aware of Bill giving her another worried glance.

She mustn't let him suspect. She sat back, passing a hand across her forehead as if her headache were still bothering her. She needed time to decide what to do next, she thought. A hundred thousand dollars! But where would she go? How could she manage to hide all by herself? But all that money! She had Bill repeat for a third time everything that had happened in that crumby little grocery store. It still made no sense to her. She saw it was beginning to be only an amusing episode to Bill. Evidently that grocer's daughter had been traveling around. One of her jealous screwball friends had been waiting to let her and any boy friend walking in with her have it. That was how Bill was putting it together. He had simply walked into something.

Alma couldn't ask him more questions. Something, she knew, had gone frightfully wrong. But she did have the money! It was hers now, if only she had enough courage. All that money! She couldn't think; she needed time. She heard Bill telling her what that lemon-haired girl had said. Alma glanced at her watch. It was nearly one. How quickly time had gone! She felt faint. Oh, God, if only she could have the courage. They were driving past a sign board with a large wooden figure of an English gentleman wearing a monocle in his eye, and a cane. The advertisement caught Alma's eyes: *Crabtree's, Ltd., the Finest Men's Store in the West. Omaha, Nebraska. 49 Miles.*

Omaha was only forty-nine miles away. They were getting to the edge of the Iowa line much too quickly. Omaha was just across the Missouri River from Council Bluffs, Iowa. In another hour they'd be in Council Bluffs and Bill would be leaving her, going on his way. What would she do, by herself? If she could only have time to think, half an hour or so of respite! Her head was really beginning to ache.

"Bill," she said suddenly. "I'm getting hungry. How about you?"

She saw she had embarrassed him. He didn't want to take money from her. He was afraid she was going to offer to buy him lunch.

"I don't usually eat at lunchtime," he said. "I'll stop at the next town, if you want. I'll be glad to wait."

"Now, Bill," she said, "don't be silly. I'll bet you're starving. Let's do this. I haven't had a picnic for ages. Can't we stop off somewhere to get some bread and cheese and milk? That would be fun. Then—let's take one of those side roads and sorta loaf our way along. After missing granny, I'm no longer in a hurry. If we could find some nice grassy place somewhere, maybe I could kill this headache."

He parked in front of a grocery store at the next town, and she had to be very serious and solemn to persuade him to take five dollars. "Now, Bill," she said. "This is my treat. Please don't be silly about it."

She sat there shivering, with all the bright June sunlight shimmering down around the Plymouth. What would she do at Council Bluffs? She mustn't forget that bridge between Council Bluffs and Omaha. Coppers would certainly be on the bridge, stopping, and possibly searching all cars. Even with the Iowa sheriff's sticker the Plymouth's windshield, it might not be enough to prevent Omaha coppers from searching. She would have to get rid of this Plymouth, somehow, if she really meant to have a try at that hundred thousand. She mustn't use the hot money, either. She would have to wait until she got safely out of the country and the heat died off before starting to cash in on that hundred grand.

She'd have to get as far west as possible, to San Francisco, and take a job there for six months or so under some false name, establishing herself under that name until she jumped north again into Canada and lost herself a second time, under a second false name. The real danger would be the long jump west, if anybody began trying to track her down.

As she waited those five or so minutes for Bill, her mind went turning and twisting. In Council Bluffs she ought to be able to get a second-hand car cheap. She had saved twenty-one hundred dollars, thank God, of her own money. She mustn't keep the Plymouth. Gramma might trace her, if Gramma was still hulking around somewhere. Maybe Monk had given her a phony pickup station. She didn't know. She certainly didn't know. It was a dead end to think about that. The money! She had to cling to that and how to get away with it. But that damned bridge between Council Bluffs and Omaha! She felt a cold hard spot grow in her mind. Couldn't she express the leather bag to herself to some city farther west, maybe Denver? Why not? Then Bill and she could drive west?

She was thinking of Bill again. She did need him. She wouldn't have the courage to go that distance by herself, thinking hour after hour of somebody possibly following her. It was such a temptation to have Bill go with her. It would be a small risk for him, too. He did want to get to Sacramento. It would almost be doing him a favor. Why not? Could she persuade him, though? She had so little time in which to do it. She mustn't arouse any suspicions. If only she had known him three or four more days. She felt a jerking sensation, seeing Bill emerge from the store, carrying a brown paper bag in his arms. He was smiling. How much he resembled Dale, she thought, and she felt a sudden pang.

Bill said, "Here's your change, Miss Lathrop. I spent a dollar and twenty-six cents."

His careful honesty went to her heart. He would be someone whom she could trust. And he could easily pass as her brother.

She smiled. "Thanks, Bill. My headache's already beginning to feel better. Let's get off somewhere and give ourselves some extra time. I'll still be able to get to Granny in Council Bluffs by three."

He turned off at the next road, going due south; the road meandered along pleasantly, eventually going west in the direction of Council Bluffs. A small stream sparkled and flowed at the left of the county road, and the day couldn't be better. He was hungry. He felt an empty sensation and was glad

Alma had wanted to stop off somewhere to have a picnic lunch. He couldn't keep from glancing at her. How pretty she was! He was pleased that her grandmother and Alma had missed connections at that crumby little grocery store. He wished the day would never end.

They drove past a sign saying: *Cold Spring Public Camp*. The dirt road wound along a grass hill covered with wild shrubs and dogwood and dandelions. Bill noticed an old table under a tree which looked like it had been through a dozen winters.

"What about here?" Alma said.

It looked wonderful to him. He parked the Plymouth under one of the trees. Below, a grassy slope ran down to the little stream. On the other side was an old fence with four cows in the pasture beyond. Birds were singing in all the trees. It was so early in the summer that the slope wasn't littered with the usual picnic rubbish of broken dishes, beer bottles, and tin cans.

Bill picked up the bag of food and milk, and waited for Alma. She opened the door on her side, the warm summer breeze blowing her skirt against her legs. She said crossly, "Bill, I haven't left this car since early this morning. Go down to the stream will you? Find us a place. I'll be there in a minute."

He stood there, looking puzzled, and her cross look changed suddenly into a smile. "Bill," she explained, "a girl has to have privacy now and then. So go on down, will you?"

He went through the trees and bushes, leaving her there. This feeling of tension would come and it would go, he knew. He would begin thinking of her as somebody helpless and fragile, about his age, even younger. Then all at once he'd be brought up sharply. He doubted if she even knew she was doing it. She was only four years older than he was, but that didn't mean she could speak to him in that kindly and infuriatingly superior fashion as if he was only ten, and she could tell him to run along now because Alma wants privacy. She wouldn't speak to him that way if he was her own age or older. Why was he only eighteen?

The three brown cows silently looked at him from across the fence, and the brown and white heifer ran along excitedly as if she expected him to come over and chase her. He said disgustedly, "Go to hell." He took off his windbreaker, spreading it on the grass for Alma when she arrived, and sat near the little stream. The water, almost up to the grassy banks from the rains, bubbled cheerfully.

He broke the loaf of bread in half. He sliced five slices of cheese with his knife. He was hungry but he waited for Alma. He rolled up his sleeves, wishing he could remove his shirt because it was very warm here on the grassy slope under the high June sun. He opened his collar and pulled down his tie and for the first time had a chance to look at it. He began smiling. It was really quite a tie. On the pale green background of the silk about a dozen little figures had been painted there in five or six colors. Each figure was the figure of the same girl, all in miniature, and as cute as a bug's ear. From head to toe, no figure was more than an inch long.

It wasn't until Bill began examining the tie that he saw each little figure was a perfect representation of a girl with a mass of chestnut hair, big shoulders, an absurdly small waist, well-rounded hips, and legs so long they were out of proportion. There was something very familiar about the miniature figures, too. It came to him all at once. They were reproductions of Fancy McMerry, the girl in the uncomic comic strip, Mr. Future.

He remembered reading in one of those glossy men's magazines you read in barbershops that the latest thing in men's hand-painted ties was to have comic-strip girls on them. However, as a tie it was a bit amusing when you took time to study it. He could understand why, after buying it for her brother-in-law, Alma must have decided not to give it to her brother-in-law, after all. Still, it was quite a tie. It was the first hand-painted tie he ever had worn.

Alma came down the hill; and he turned, watching her. She was carrying her camel's-hair coat slung carelessly over one shoulder. She saw Bill had spread his wind-breaker on the grass for her and she sat gracefully on it, one leg bent under the other, casually dropping her own coat to one side. She had a nice trim figure. Nicely proportioned, compact and neat, as if it all belonged there and hadn't been padded.

She said, "Am I hungry! Let's eat."

The bread was fresh. The cheese was good. The milk was rich and creamy. But she didn't appear to be very hungry after all, and only picked at her food; he ate his whole share and more. After he finished, he still felt hungry. He was going to have to learn to tighten his belt, he guessed, until he got to Sacramento and had a job there and money coming in.

"How's your headache?"

"Oh, much better, thanks. I'm thirsty, though. That water looks nice and cool."

"I'll get you some."

He walked to the little stream a few yards down the incline, kneeling to fill an empty milk carton with water. The skittish brown and white heifer directly across the stream mooed at him more vigorously. The three brown cows observed without interest, their jaws moving in steady rhythm. When he returned, Alma was slightly alarmed. "Those cows won't break through and come over, will they?"

He said, "They can't get through the fence. Even if they could they wouldn't harm anyone."

She drank the water. "Gosh, it's good. It's suddenly good to be alive, isn't it? I'm going to take off these nylons and start tanning my legs."

She turned her back to him while she stripped off her stockings. Her legs were a creamy white, shapely, and tapered just right at the ankles. She slipped on her shoes, wadding up the nylons and stuffing them in a coat pocket. She opened her leather purse and scowled at herself in a little mirror. "My, I look like a hag. I was in such a hurry this morning I left my powder and lipstick."

"You look beautiful to me, Miss Lathrop."

"You look beautiful to me," he had told her. That was better, even if she had had to fish for it.

She let herself turn to him, smiling. She mustn't show too much leg. A little wouldn't hurt. He kept reminding her more and more of Dale. Dale, though, would have had his hand reaching for her by now. She shivered, then composed herself and leaned forward and said earnestly:

"Now, Bill. Let's not be so formal. I'm Alma. And please don't ever give a girl that line." Why, he was blushing! It made him look incredibly young. She continued, gravely and sweetly, "I know I've got looks. My gracious! A girl with any looks at all has been told that by hundreds of guys. That's no compliment. Ask a girl what kind of lipstick she uses. So you remember and one day buy one for her as a present. She says, 'Oh, darling!' That's how you get a girl to kiss you without making a pass at her." She grinned.

"What's yours, Miss Lathrop?" He was smiling.

"Alma," she reminded him. "It's Revlon's Pink Fire."

They both laughed. Despite his shyness he had taken her up quickly enough on that. Oh, hell. If only he was four years older than she was instead of four years younger. But all her time was running out. She had to get to Council Bluffs, express the money, buy a second-hand car, and somehow get the Plymouth out of sight, and persuade Bill to meet her and go on with her. She felt her heart thumping. Oh, God, why didn't he make a play for her and give her a chance to suggest that he drive with her to the coast? It was probably because she was older. He was decent and nice and trying to be so very proper with her. For an instant something wild and inflamed seemed to course through her veins. He was so much like Dale! She wanted of a sudden to run her hands through that close-cropped tow hair of his and fondle him and love him until he felt the excitement she was beginning to feel; and then the coldness again came on her. She was a fool. One hundred grand! If ever he guessed what a little tramp she was at heart she would never have a chance to persuade him to drive west with her. She wondered how much experience he had had with girls. Probably, she thought, not very much. But even if he was young, he was like young hickory, all lean and strong, waiting to be aroused. But she must be the rich young college girl with him, the young lady, casual, cool, but definitely thinking of continuing west.

She said, "Bill, you know what? Maybe it's fate or something, the two of us running into each other like this . . ."

He gave her a quick glance. She had so little time. She was afraid she was rushing it. But she must go on.

"I should have told you sooner," she said in a soft clear voice, "but I live in California, you know. I live there with my sister in San Francisco. She's all I have, except Granny."

"You live in California?"

That was an eager, hopeful look he'd flashed at her. God, the idea had come to him before she had had to say it. At least he was taken by her. She was thankful for her good looks.

"I hate driving by myself," she told him. "Usually, I go home by plane after school gets out. But Granny let me use her car this year. She promised I could drive all the way to San Francisco and I was looking forward to it, too. But, somehow, I don't know . . ." She let her voice trail off, watching him from under her silky lashes. He was gazing back at her, sitting up erectly. The idea was beginning to come more strongly to him. Then she said, being the old lady of fifty and very, very sensible, "I hate driving by myself. I can see, too, you're very trustworthy, Bill. It's not as if you were my age, either. Being younger sorta—sort of makes it like I was an older sister. It might be fun to have you drive me to California if you liked."

He was startled. He couldn't quite believe she was serious.

He said, "Us—two?"

"Yes, silly." She gave him a grave look. "What's wrong with that?"

"Nothing—"

"All right. Don't look so surprised. I'd be afraid, driving alone. I wouldn't, with you along. I'd pay you—"

"Wait a minute, Miss Lathrop—"

"Alma," she interrupted, smiling.

He swallowed. It was incredible. All the way to California! He said, "I wouldn't want pay, Alma."

"That's better. Now, listen. Bill. Let's be sensible. I'd want to pay you. Don't be hurt at what I'm going to say, will you?"

He didn't know what she was going to say. He would do anything to have the chance of driving her to California.

"I mean," she continued, "after all, I *am* four years older than you are. If you were my age, well—you know—it would be different, wouldn't it?"

Bill felt his face redden. He did know what she meant. After all, a girl of twenty-two couldn't very well pick up with some strange man her age or older and start driving across the country with him. But it would be different if she drove west, he could see from her point of view, and decided to pick up an eighteen-year-old kid. Bill knew it was different even if he resented it because it was different. Why should the age differential mean so much? Actually, it didn't. He knew that, too. He was eighteen and he knew that. But people got over being eighteen and forgot, and they didn't know and thought it was different.

"Bill, please." She was being much older than he was and very sensible. "I'd want it like that. To be terribly frank, I wouldn't want to feel I was under any obligation to you after we got there. I'd drop you off in Sacramento. I'd go on to meet my sister. On the way we'd probably have to stop at motels. Even if we don't look anything alike, at least our hair and eyes are close to the same color. We could say we were sister and brother so—" she faltered charmingly, "—so nobody at motels would start talking if we had adjoining rooms."

That much of it made sense to Bill. He still didn't want to accept any pay, though. She was watching him, with almost a tense look about her, he felt. Her face was no longer pale, and her eyes were bright. When she took a quick breath he could not help noticing the delight of her slim body under that pull-over. Her eyes were of the deepest blue. Her lips were softly curved, and when she leaned toward him and a capricious summer breeze puffed a light skein of her hair against his temple, it was all he could do not to take her in his arms. His heart was hammering. But if she even guessed how he was beginning to feel, it would ruin all his chances at this wonderful, this incredibly wonderful piece of luck offered to him. Because he was four years younger, evidently she felt very secure with him. Well, she would be safe with him, he told himself angrily. He felt a rush of gratitude for her unexpected kindness. He'd kill himself, first, before ever she regretted her unexpected offer.

"Alma, I can't think of anything I'd like more than to drive you to the coast, if you mean it."

"I mean it."

She pressed his hand in a quick friendly gesture. He had never had such luck. He had looked forward to long days on the road west. Instead he ought to be in Sacramento by early next week. Best of all, Alma would be with him all the way. He hoped she wasn't joking with him. No, he was certain she meant it. There was one thing, though, she was saying. She didn't want Bill to have his feelings hurt, either. But if he wouldn't accept pay, she'd like to buy him a present. "I'd want to pay you by having you buy something nice for yourself in Council Bluffs when I stop at Granny's. Now please. Let's not—"

She looked away, startled. Her fingers tightened around his wrist. She pointed with her other hand. "Look, Bill. Isn't that a bull? Maybe we'd better get out of here. I'd hate to have him get across at us. I'm not much of a country girl, I'm afraid."

Unnoticed, a great black bull had come down over the hill toward the cows. Bill hastily decided it was time for Alma and himself to return to the car. He wasn't afraid of the bull. He knew there wasn't any danger to Alma or himself. That wasn't it.

The bull had a bloody strip of flesh hanging from his leathery nose. It meant that the bull had caught wind of the skittish black and white heifer, and had broken loose from the nose ring to come down over the hill after her. Probably the farmer who owned the black bull didn't even know the bull had broken through from somewhere beyond the hill and was in here, attracted by the young heifer. The bull had pushed his way through the three sedate older cows and was already butting at the young heifer. Bill had been so intent listening to Alma that he hadn't noticed the bull. He had lived long enough on a farm to know what was coming next.

Bill said quietly, "I guess we'd better be on our way."

He never finished. Alma grasped more tightly at his wrist, restraining him. She was watching the bull. "Honey, look . . ."

She started to giggle. Then she bent forward from her hips, as if all of her was drawn by what was so suddenly happening on the other side of the stream and fence. Her face was smoothed out into a blank beauty, her eyes round, her lips parting, with her teeth showing, small and white.

Bill had started to rise, but he stayed where he was, as if caught himself. He had more an awareness of Alma than of what was over there on the other side of the fence. The sky spun in a bright blueness. Bill felt Alma's hand clinging to his. Alma gasped softly, and from somewhere beyond the stream and fence there was a sound of hoofs stamping and then the heifer suddenly mooed and the black bull was away from her, panting heavily.

Bill looked at Alma, and she turned her head and looked at him and her face was a rosy color. Her lips were stretched pinkly across the white even teeth. As she tried to get her breath, her small breasts pushed out, shallow and round, against the knitted fabric of the yellow pullover. To Bill's eyes her hair was like soft thick corn silk. Her bare knees were round and smooth where, unnoticed by her, her skirt and white nylon slip had pulled up.

He had a sensation of straining as she was straining. It was hard to breathe. He pulled her toward him. She yielded. He wanted her terribly. Nothing else mattered. She was so lovely. He felt her withdraw her hand from his and then, unexpectedly, her hand went out to him. His heart gave a lurch. For an instant he could not move, with a kind of horrifying delight flaming up through him like sudden fire.

Her face flamed. Snatching away her hand, she jumped up and ran rapidly away from him, running like a young deer.

Chapter Six

She drove half blinded by tears. She didn't know why she didn't give the wheel a twist and go off the road and hope she broke her neck. Everything had been going along so smoothly, too. Oh, hell, what was wrong with her? It had welled up in her all at once and she hadn't been able to help herself. She was worse than any heifer. Time and time again she'd resolved to be finished with that sort of thing and to make a fresh start somewhere, thousands of miles away, and learn to be decent—like those college girls she had met back in Des Moines at the beauty shop.

She had even nerved herself to the big jump of taking all of that money. A hundred thousand dollars! Now what was she gonna do? You fool, she thought. She took another turn in the winding road, the sun spattering down in light and shade on the dusty road through the overhanging boughs of trees. She couldn't do it alone. There was that bridge that connected Omaha and Council Bluffs. Coppers would probably search the Plymouth. Bill had wanted to go with her, too. It had been nearly arranged, except for his payment for the driving. She *wanted* to buy him something, too. He deserved that much from her. He had refused any money. While he was taking the Plymouth to Omaha and buying himself a suit, she would have had time to do what was necessary if she expected really to vanish so deeply and so far away that nobody—Gramma, Monk, if he escaped the dragnet—nobody at all, ever would see her again. Having Bill drive the blue Plymouth into Omaha, too, would spot the car there if anyone had an eye for that car after it crossed into Nebraska.

What was she to do? The question drummed into her frantic mind. She slowed down, the coldness taking hold of her. What a fool she was! She felt the steering wheel waver in her hands. Hastily, she clamped on the brakes. She had a sensation of the entire valley and hill tilting slowly and then receding again.

She had left her coat back there. Poor Bill. She smiled ruefully to herself, sitting back in the seat and deliberately forcing herself to take long deep breaths. She had tried to be the pure young little lady with Bill. And she had almost succeeded, too. He was nice. How strong he was, too. You wouldn't believe he was only an eighteen-year-old kid—

She stopped the drifting of her thoughts along that sort of thing, right there. A hundred thousand dollars! She placed her hands to her burning cheeks. She needed Bill. She could say something, try to explain. She hated herself. She wouldn't hurt him. He did want to go to California. Imagine that rotten uncle of his, stealing all of Bill's insurance! It wasn't fair for Bill to have to try to hitch-hike all that distance to Sacramento. And as long as he was driving with her she was certain she'd be safe. They would simply be a sister and a younger brother, driving together. She would have to go back. She would think of something to explain to him, she told herself. She had to.

Bill's heart was trying to knock itself out of his chest. He got up slowly. He had a light-headed sensation, from what she'd done, the tension, and probably also from lack of enough food. She had already vanished when he sighted up toward the trees hiding the road. He slung his old windbreaker over a shoulder, picked up her coat, and started up the slope. Halfway to the road he heard the sudden thrumming of the Plymouth's engine as she drove away, leaving him behind.

He was transfixed. She'd left him here, stranded. Well, to hell with her. How badly she'd taken him in! He'd been on her side. He'd wanted to help her. She was a poor rich girl who deserved sympathy. He hadn't believed her when she'd said candidly she was spoiled and selfish.

Sweat was on his face. His heart was still pounding like a trip hammer when all reason for it pounding so violently had ended.

The hollow space increased inside his stomach. He lurched a little. He didn't know what had come over her or him, seeing that bull and heifer. He'd never had a thing like that happen to him before. For a minute or so Alma had wanted him, too. It was why she'd run away. She'd driven off in what must have been a whole convulsion of nerves, leaving him stranded.

With a heaviness not usual for him, he continued up the slope. He was reminded of how it had been that hot afternoon last summer with Thelma Binns. Thelma, too, had shoved him off at the last minute with a confusing kind of prudery and rage, at herself more than him, mixed with something which had almost been a compassion for him. He had always assumed that the man made the advances and the girl retreated. It was true enough, only too true, he knew, with the half a dozen girls of his graduating class whom he had liked and who had always had a sort of wariness about him and any of the other fellows.

He wished he was older. It was so perplexing. It was humiliating, too. Perhaps last summer he should have forced Thelma to go on. It had been the same thing all over again, not so many minutes ago, with Alma. He felt himself begin to tremble all over, even at the thought of it. He probably would have made a fool of himself, too. An older girl always had an edge on you.

It had been a pipe dream, anyway, he decided, to hope to drive with her to California. She had even warned him about herself. She was one of those rich screwball girls who did the first thing that entered their heads, were ashamed of themselves the next second, and went running off. Good riddance. He wondered how far from the main highway he was. He listened. He couldn't even hear Alma's Plymouth now. She must have driven away like a bat out of hell. He found he was feeling sorry for her, and that was being stupid.

He threw his knapsack over one shoulder, her camel's-hair coat over the other. He felt his feet leadenly hitting the dusty road. Well, he had got this far. He could get the rest of the way. He should have known better than to let himself build such high hopes. He halted, hearing the sound of a car's engine swelling in the distance. A hundred yards to the south the road curved off to the west. If a car was coming it would be coming in the wrong direction for him to hope for a ride to Council Bluffs. Still, it might give him a chance to be carried as far as the main highway, fifteen or so miles to the north.

He was dumfounded when he saw the Plymouth reappear. Alma's head leaned out the window as she backed the car toward him. It came completely around the curve. She saw him, the Plymouth stopped. Her face squeezed together pitifully, like a child's. She didn't call to him.

He took long strides toward the Plymouth, slowing as he approached. He felt like an awkward intruder. He was convinced she had returned for her coat. Silently, he held it out to her. She didn't speak or move to extend an arm through the car window for it. "Here," he said.

Instead of accepting it, she said wretchedly, "Bill, I'm so ashamed of myself. I never had anything like that happen to me before. I just don't know why I—I—" Tears blurred her eyes. "What must you think of me?"

She hadn't returned for her coat. She had returned for him! He had been wrong in everything he'd angrily thought about her when he believed that she'd run off for good.

"Alma, it could happen to anybody."

"Honest?"

"Honest, Alma."

She opened the door on his side. "If you don't think I'm so awful . . . Gosh, Bill. Get in, will you?"

It was what he wanted to hear her say. It was wonderful to know she had returned for him, after all. He got behind the wheel while she folded her coat on the shelf next to her neat canvas suitcase with the Drake U sticker on it. At the next crossroads a sign invited you to stop at the Old Steamboat Motel, one mile east of Council Bluffs, and told you Council Buffs was thirty-four miles away.

He said, "Council Bluffs?" not daring to ask her if she still hoped to have him drive her west.

Probably she had changed her mind after what had happened back there.

"Oh, Bill," she said unhappily, "I still feel so cheap."

"It was my fault. When I saw that bull . . ."

"Honest, if a girl and boy just happen to be there when—?"

He was leaving part of it unsaid and so was she. The Plymouth rushed over a wooden bridge.

"It's awful," Alma said after a silence. "Why, it's like learning you're an animal, yourself, capable of being excited just like an animal even if you don't want to be." She shivered. "Bill, I've got to say something and then we'll stop talking about it."

When he took an instant to glance at her he saw her face was all pale again. He wanted to tell her to stop berating herself. It wasn't that important.

"I couldn't have you drive me across the continent if you had wrong ideas about me, Bill."

"I haven't. It was my fault—"

"I liked good times with boys at Drake. But I've just got to tell you I haven't ever been intimate with any boy. Maybe if I had I wouldn't have had that horrible wish come over me back there." Her voice stopped. "Anyway, I don't care if it sounds old-fashioned," she said defiantly. "I've promised myself to wait until I'm married. There! I expect you've had all sorts of girls. It's only fair to tell you if we can't drive to California and just be friends, nothing more, you'd best get out at Council Bluffs."

"Alma," he murmured, greatly moved. He wanted to drive with her to California. He wanted her to know he respected her and liked her. "Alma, I haven't had any girls like that, either."

"Why, Bill. Some girls would throw themselves at somebody as nice and tall and good-looking as you."

"You don't know my uncle. He was strict as a preacher. Besides, most of the girls I knew were nice girls, like you. They wouldn't throw themselves at anybody without a marriage license."

"Bill, honey, I'm glad you told me. I wish you really were my brother. A sister can help a brother because she knows so much more about girls than a boy. Boys are so shy the first time they usually go to some tramp, just giving herself to anyone and not caring. It shouldn't be like that. It should be nice and wonderful. I'm so happy you're waiting until someday you find the right girl. I know she'll make you glad you did wait, too. Now let's just not talk about it, ever again. Is that a bargain?"

Everything was all right, once more, even if she had misunderstood the reason he had waited. He hadn't knowingly been waiting for a little Miss Right. The real reason was humiliating and intolerable. It was because the town was so small and his uncle had been so obsessed. Last summer Bill had tried to tell Thelma Binns, after playing tennis with her. His telling had failed, ending in a crushing frustration for them both. At least, Alma had been more sympathetic and understanding. He wasn't too displeased for having given in to an impulse to share his secret with her. She hadn't thought it humorous or unmanly of him because he was eighteen, nearly, and was still inexperienced. Rather, she'd appeared pleased. He promised himself he was going to think of her as an older sister, not too much older, but old enough to have it stay like this between them all across the continent.

He nodded. "It's a bargain, Alma."

"We'll have three or four heavenly days, going to California. You'll be my nice younger brother. Now, go faster! I want to finish everything I have to do in Council Bluffs quickly, so we can be fifty or a hundred miles west in Nebraska before having to stop for the night."

It was too risky to drive much faster than fifty miles an hour on the narrow, winding county road. Now that it was all settled and they were really going west together, Bill was determined to prove to Alma he was a good driver. He had no intention of having an accident, not if he could help it.

They drove through Griswold. At the end of town a police officer flagged them down, saw the sticker in the-lower left-hand corner of the windshield, and wearily waved them to keep on. After that the road carried them straight toward Council Bluffs with no more obstructions.

She had done it, she thought, sitting there quietly in the seat and being careful, too, not to sit too close to him. She should have been an actress, she thought bitterly. But what chance had she ever had to be much of anything, until now?

Bill's renewed excitement at the chance of continuing to California with her was once more exciting her. It gave her the strangest glow, too. She had better take hold of herself. She was going to have her chance, at last. All that money! She could get away. She could get a new start. If a fella made a pass at her she'd give her head a toss, like those cute college girls always did back in Des Moines. She could be as decent and, sorta gay, as they were, once she got so far away fellas like Monk would never find her. Bill was somebody good for her, too. What luck it was, happening on him! She saw more billboard signs rush by. They were getting closer to Council Bluffs. The Lemore Hotel in Council Bluffs promised the newest beds. A beer sign advertised creamy beer, made right in Omaha. There was another one of those Crabtree clothing-store signs, too, with the mileage to Omaha, fourteen miles. Only fourteen miles!

That bridge connecting Council Bluffs to Omaha haunted her. She had to persuade Bill to drive the Plymouth over that bridge and arrange to meet him in Omaha after she had completed everything she had to do in Council Bluffs. She slanted her eyes at him, remembering to smile. She did want to do something nice for him, too. She began talking to him about buying a new suit, while a part of her mind went racing away toward the future. One hundred thousand dollars! She could get away. Look how she had managed with Bill. Nothing now connected her to Monk or Gramma, either. Even if the police had pounced upon both of them, they wouldn't squeal. She was certain of that.

She could get away, if only she would hold on to herself a few more hours and manage everything without a slip. That leather bag of money! She couldn't keep Bill with her while she expressed that bag as far as Denver, addressing it to herself, and got a cheap car.

"Oh, Bill, it'll be heavenly having someone drive me home. I hate driving alone. If you won't accept pay you must let me do something—don't be sore at what I'm going to say. If we're going to go across the continent together as brother and sister, it would look sort of funny, wouldn't it, if you were dressed like you are now when I've got these clothes on? I do like wearing nice clothes. I'd want to pay you by having you buy a suit or a nice sport coat and slacks. Please!"

His face got hard and he shook his head. She was at her most charming best. When he walked in to ask for a part time job at that Sacramento newspaper, wouldn't it help if he was nicely dressed? If he wished, he could call it a loan. He wanted that job, didn't he?

"It would be a loan?"

"Yes, of course. My heavens, Bill. Don't be so stubborn." She looked at her watch. "Now, listen. I've got to stop at Granny's a little while and scold her for not waiting for me at Atlantic. You can wait that long?"

"Anything you want, Alma," he assured her.

He was calling her "Alma," too, as she had asked. She did like him. He was strong and big and honest and it would give her such a sense of protection to have him along. It wouldn't be a risk for him, either, if everything worked out as she believed it would. A hundred thousand dollars! Hawaii! Anywhere in the world! She gave a start. He was asking where her grandmother lived in Council Bluffs? Then she saw one of the hotel signs flashing by: Hotel St. George. Of course. That was where her grandmother lived.

The Hotel St. George was of brick, painted white, with green shutters. In the entrance was standing a doorman, looking uncomfortable and too warm with epaulets and gold braid. Bill had assumed he was to wait here in the Plymouth until she had finished with her phoning and explaining to her grandmother, but Alma surprised him. "Silly," she said, "do I have to draw a picture for you? I know I can trust you. But Granny's kinda old and not too awfully broad-minded. I'd just as soon let her think I'm going to California by myself, not with somebody I kinda fell for." She smiled at him.

He hadn't thought that an older person might be very dubious about Alma driving off to California with some young stranger she'd picked up along the road. It was as if, somehow, he was engaged with Alma in something that was not quite respectable. But that wasn't true. His mind was still going around in a whirl. He couldn't quite believe Alma had actually decided to have him drive her to California. His main desire, though, was to get to Sacramento. Obviously Alma was one of the rich girls who did as they pleased. He was lucky to have such a break. He was not even consciously aware that he had compromised for what was expedient, going against a small warning in his mind.

She had asked him to hand her her bag and her suitcase. What bag? He had only seen that suitcase with the Drake U sticker on it. Silly. She had her old shabby leather bag down behind the seat. It was so shabby looking she had been ashamed of it. She'd probably leave it here with granny. All it had was some junk in it, her books and stuff, from Drake. So he reached down and pulled up the bag and it was heavy, and he handed her the bag and suitcase. The doorman was waiting now, very polite, a general in a green uniform.

Bill felt the heat inside the Plymouth. It was hot and muggy in the city, so near the Missouri river. The general in a green uniform carried away the two bags. Alma had opened her leather purse.

"Listen, Bill," she said with an air of great practicality. "Do something to please me? Don't waste time looking for a suit in one of these crummy stores. Go across the river to Omaha. Find a smart store there."

She recalled all the signs on the highway. Yes, and Monk had said something about it being the best store in Omaha. "Go to Crabtree's, in Omaha, Bill. Some of the Drake boys I knew who lived in Omaha always went to Crabtree's. Can you remember? I'll tell you. Get either a gabardine suit or a nice tweed jacket and gray slacks. Get something you can be proud of wearing when you're walking into that Sacramento newspaper to ask for a job. Will you?"

When she looked at you, the pink lips smiling, the blue eyes so earnest, her dark-blonde hair skinned back from her curving forehead, it was like seeing a warm-hearted friend a few years older who enjoyed giving you a friendly hand. After all, it was a loan. First appearances did count, too, when you hunted a job. But his stomach began cramping.

"Where'll we meet? I've never been in Omaha."

"Oh, gosh, I've only passed through it myself."

"All cities have public libraries. How about on the steps of the Omaha public library?"

"Wonderful! I don't know how long I'll be with Granny. Let's make it five o'clock. Take all the time you need. Oh, Bill, I'm so excited, knowing we'll soon be driving west. Here, buy a nice suit—" She thrust a wad of bills in his hand, blew him a kiss, and ran toward the hotel.

Bill unfolded the crumpled bills. There were fifty-dollar bills, three of them. It was the first time in his life he'd ever seen fifty-dollar bills. He'd agreed he was to borrow only fifty dollars from her. He moved across the seat peering out, feeling the heat strike at him. Alma had vanished inside the hotel. The doorman returned to say politely, "I'm sorry, sir. But there's no parking allowed here. If you wish to wait there's a convenient parking lot for our guests directly behind the hotel. Shall I park it for you?"

Bill said no, never mind. When next he saw Alma he would have to have some sort of understanding with her. Even if she was loaded with money, he didn't want her to think—he didn't know quite how to express it to himself. By asking the traffic officer at the first intersection he was directed toward the bridge. He could see you had to pay one way or another when you accepted a free ride across the continent, if only in self-pride. He wanted to get to Sacramento. He had been prepared himself to go the hard way. He'd do the driving for Alma. It would be a small return for her favors, but at least it would be an attempt at doing his share. He didn't know precisely how she placed him, probably in a category more or less of a hired chauffeur and attendant. Well, that was fair enough. He could smell the hot thick air blowing off the river, mixed in with the smell of hot asphalt pavements. It was turning into a real scorcher down here in the river valley.

Cars were lining up waiting to pay toll charges on the bridge. Two state officers were passing from car to car questioning the occupants. One came to Bill. But the other said, "This one's already been passed, Fred. He's got a sheriff's sticker on the windshield. Take the next car."

Bill shoved his head through the window, asking what all the trouble was. The state cop nearest him said, "Bub, I ain't the public information department. Pay your toll. Can't you see you're holding up the line?"

So Bill paid the toll, crossed into Omaha, and drove through the drab hot stink of that part of the city near the river. A hollow feeling inside him increased. The sunlight sparkled like sharp diamonds on the windshield, glaring into his eyes. His head began throbbing a little.

He turned into a parking lot. It was fifty cents for three hours. That was all right. Bill was rich. He could have paid a dollar. He could have paid ten dollars. This morning he'd started off with twenty-two dollars. Alma had shoved three fifty-dollar bills at him as if they were nothing to her. She should have known better, she did need someone to look after her. The parking lot man said the public library was about ten blocks west and three to the east. He wasn't too certain. He had a map. He could look it up.

Bill said, "Thanks. I'll find it."

Chapter Seven

Probably he could have found a parking lot closer to the public library. But while he had been in the Plymouth, for no particular reason, he had felt that it was carrying him on and controlling his movements. When he began hitting the cement sidewalk with his feet he felt he could stop when and where he wanted to stop and take over for himself again.

He bought an afternoon paper from the newsboy on the next corner. The left-hand column was about the heat wave. At twelve noon, the temperature was 101 degrees, and the hospitals had reported ten cases of heat prostration, more expected.

The right-hand column was filled with details about an armored-truck robbery early this morning, near Boone, Iowa. Three guards, the driver, a state policeman, and one of the mobsters had been killed. An autopsy had indicated that the motorcycle policeman had not only been shot by machine-gun bullets from the gun of the dead mobster, but also had been riddled through the back by the armored truck's machine guns. It was assumed that the motorcycle policeman had been caught in the cross fire, dying instantly. The motorcycle policeman had not been assigned to accompany the armored truck to Boone, and it was not yet established why he had been pacing the truck. Ordinarily all shipments were made without a police escort, since it had been believed that the truck was sufficiently armored to protect its contents.

Bill's eyes skipped to a lower paragraph. The shipment of over half a million dollars had completely vanished. Over half a million dollars! Bill whistled to himself, blinking sweat from his eyelashes. That explained why all roads had been blocked into Council Bluffs. He glanced at a three-column cut of the sour heavy face of a man wearing glasses, the caption underneath asking in large type: "Have you seen this man? If so, immediately report to the nearest police. He is Monk Anzeiger, wanted for . . ."

Bill had not seen a Monk Anzeiger, wanted for participation in the holdup this morning. He never expected to, either. It was the same old story, he thought. Almost every day when you opened a newspaper the headlines were filled with someone getting away with hundreds of thousands of dollars, the police promising a quick arrest, and very seldom succeeding. It happened so often nobody seemed to care much, any more. At the end of the next block he tossed the newspaper into the big green waste container.

Before buying a gabardine suit at Crabtree's, Limited, to please Alma, he wanted to locate the public library. The library was the only remaining link to connect him back to Alma.

It was a screwy notion, maybe. That light-headed feeling was beginning to spin him a little, every now and then. But he had to see the library to make certain it really did exist. Once he found the library he would have a compass bearing of sorts. Then he would locate Crabtree's, buy the first ready-made suit that fitted him, have a big lunch, and get back to the library.

He stepped into a drugstore, one of those drugstores that sold everything but the kitchen stove. Probably you could even buy a stove if you were willing to wait ten minutes while the manager or whoever snapped his fingers had one assembled out of the Kiddie-Toy sets and the spare kerosene lamps from the homeware department.

At the right of the entrance, behind the cosmetic counter, a girl with a pug face, slanted eyes, and burgundy-red lipstick on a bored mouth, took time to explain that he crossed west through the park, continued one block, and there the public library was.

The slanted gray eyes regarded him as if she were wondering why he wanted to waste his time in a stuffy public library on a hot muggy June afternoon like this. He glanced down at a tray filled with lipsticks. It had stuck in his mind how Alma had made fun of him on that grassy slope when he'd impulsively told her she was beautiful. She'd remarked calmly if he wished to compliment a girl he should remember her favorite lipstick and give her one as a surprise. He had twenty-two dollars of his own, which he had earned. He wanted very much to buy Alma a gift, with his own money, not with the hundred and fifty dollars which Alma had thrust into his hands. Whatever money of that he spent to buy himself a suit he was determined he would pay back to her, as soon as he got a job in Sacramento.

When he asked the girl behind the cosmetic counter if she sold Revlon lipstick her smile implied a man might not know it, but she had carloads, simply carloads of genuine Revlon lipsticks. If she wished she could press an invisible button and out they would pop in all sizes and colors, glittering with diamonds and rubies and precious gems.

"What shade?" she asked, the slanted eyes regarding him. There were a million shades, the tone of her voice suggested. She had all day. She could play guessing games with him. But he'd never guess the right shade.

"I'd like 'Pink Fire', please," he said.

She appeared pleased. He could imagine her thinking that he had reached out to catch the brass ring on the first try around. Her temples were moist. Small beads of perspiration had collected in the hollow of her throat. The afternoon was turning unpleasantly sultry, and the heat and humidity and lack of food were giving him the damnedest notions.

The girl was showing him a dozen genuine "Pink Fire" Revlon lipsticks. They cost from a dollar and a quarter to two dollars, depending upon the container. He wanted Alma to have the very best. Now that he was away from her he couldn't cease thinking of her. He was already missing her. It was as if he had known her for years. This pug-faced girl with the slanted eyes wasn't half as pretty as Alma was. He asked if there were more expensive containers, and she answered, "Why yes, indeed," eying him as if he'd graduated to the top of the class. One of the deluxe containers of genuine plated gold would cost ten dollars and twenty-two cents. There would be a slight delay while the 'Pink Fire' shade was fitted into a genuine deluxe container.

He had two hours to kill until he saw Alma. It was an eternity. He had better stop thinking so much about her. Perhaps he shouldn't-have bought her such an expensive present. Hell, there was nothing wrong in buying her a lipstick. He gave the girl eleven dollars, his own money, all one-dollar bills. It would be less than ten minutes to wait, she said. If it was all the same to her, he answered, he had an errand. He'd return, say, in an hour. It was all the same to her, tall and blond, she said.

That threw him a little, but it amused him too. It was as if after being with Alma he had somehow matured enough to know how to take another girl who was also a few years older. "Does the sweet talk go with every purchase?"

She said modestly, "The manager expects us to please all our customers. Don't you like being called 'tall and blond?'"

He entered into it. "I thought I brushed the hay off before I walked in."

Unexpectedly she smiled, and stopped joking with him. "I *was* fresh, wasn't I? That tan gives you away. It's not a city tan. It's the kind of tan I used to have on my old man's farm before I decided to be a city girl. I guess it's the humidity. On afternoons like this I go slightly crazy, don't you?"

"I feel as if the top of my head's lifting a couple of inches."

"Yeah, I know. It's—psst! That's the manager." Her voice changed.

"Anything else, sir?"

"No, thank you."

"I'll have your purchase waiting for you, sir."

It had been slightly crazy of them both but he had enjoyed it. She had something of the same good-natured sassy quality that had attracted him so strongly to Alma. Perhaps that was something all girls began acquiring after they became nineteen or twenty, and had learned to be good company and easy and casual and have fun.

He wished the time would go by faster till five o'clock. He thought of telephoning the Hotel St. George, and asking for Alma to tell her, "I'm beginning to miss you like hell." Christ, that wouldn't do! Her grandmother wasn't even supposed to know he existed. It must be the heat that gave him such a crazy happy-go-lucky sort of feeling. He stopped in the park to drink from the sanitary fountain, then changed his mind. Raspberry-colored lipstick was smeared over the nickel-plated spout.

The sky was melting copper, the air hushed and thick. Perhaps it might soon rain. He wasn't the only one in the world to have thought of the main public library as the best place to meet a friend. A gray-haired man was at one end of the steps, a large sticky looking man was mopping his face on the top row of steps, and over on the other side a girl was sitting disconsolately on a cheap suitcase, angrily tapping one shoe on the hot concrete. A rather untidy gray-haired woman hastened to the gray-haired man and said, "Harry, I couldn't get here sooner. They were having a big sale."

The girl with brassy yellow hair halfway down her back was sitting on the upended suitcase beneath a stone lion or a pigeon or a civic founder. Bill wasn't enough interested to decide what the stone statue signified. The girl had glanced at the gray-haired husband and wife; and now she happened to catch Bill's eye and half smiled and Bill half smiled back, as two strangers sometimes will do when they both see something that amuses them.

She was dressed in a tight green jacket cut to prove she was simply sensational, in the same way the Fancy McMerry girls parading in miniature on Bill's silk tie were all sensational. On a day this hot and muggy, Bill wondered why she didn't remove her jacket and cut off some of that hair. He decided she was probably twenty. Her face was pink and flushed from the heat, with a redness around her eyelids where they were beginning to sunburn. But she had quite a figure. The second man who was higher up on the steps would stare at her every now and then. Unexpectedly she asked Bill, "You haven't the time?"

That light-headed sensation kept bothering him. His wrist watch had an alarming tendency to tick slowly, very slowly, around his wrist as he looked at the time. He said politely it was fourteen minutes after three. He thought the girl was going to cry. She stamped her foot. It was ridiculous and pathetic. She was so angry at herself she didn't care if he was a perfect stranger. "I'm an hour anna half too early," she said. "That hall clock. Why don't I ever do anything right for once!"

"Tough," Bill said politely. She didn't compare at all to Alma.

"You wooden like killing an hour having a drink?" she asked. "Or are you waiting for somebody likewise?"

"More or less," Bill said. "Sorry. You wouldn't know where Crabtree's store is would you?"

"The big men's store? Sure. Across the park and two blocks to your left."

It was a torpidly hot afternoon, the heat sucking the river smell from the river and releasing it all over the city. The air seemed even hotter and thicker on this side of the street.

The sign above the entrance spelled out: "Crabtree's, Ltd., Finest Clothing for Men." He looked into one big window and saw a display of hand-painted ties, each tie carefully knotted around a waxen neck which continued up to a waxen jaw, white wax teeth, part of a waxen nose, and nothing more; the wax head had been sliced in two. A small chaste sign on a gold stand, with lion claws at each leg, read: "Your Choice of Comic-Strip Girls. Each Tie Hand-Stenciled by Hand. $25.00."

Perhaps he hadn't read the chastely printed sign correctly and "Hand" wasn't repeated there. He looked up at the large gold letters above the entrance: Crabtree's, Ltd., Store No. 6. Finest Men's Clothing. Lowest Prices. London Inspired Styling. He remembered, now, the label inside his hand-painted tie was a Crabtree's, Ltd., label. He looked into the window display again, seeing a dozen other girls from comic strips reproduced on the displayed ties. But he didn't see any Fancy McMerry such as his was. All the ties in the display, too, had only one comic-strip girl stenciled large enough to see her, not a dozen or so in miniature like the tiny reproductions romping in a swirling pattern over the rich silk knotted at his throat.

He moved on to the next window, wondering what kind of suits Crabtree's had. What he wanted was a fine suit at the lowest possible price. The hot humid air rising from the sidewalk had an unpleasant smell. Men, one or two accompanied by a woman, were passing in and out through the entrance. Evidently Crabtree's, Ltd., were doing a thriving business. He was in no hurry. His watch was correct, he wasn't a whole hour and a half ahead of the right time like that brassy-haired girl had been. Perhaps she would have known where you could buy big steak sandwiches. If only he could be certain Alma would be there at five!

In the next window was a display of men's gloves, each glove slipped over a plastic hand, the plastic arm fastened to an iron gilt rod curving from the floor like a frozen palm leaf. The sign explained the gloves were made from genuine peccary skins, and if you didn't know from what animal peccary skins came, the explanation was there to be read. They were South American pigs. How interesting. Bill wasn't very fascinated, though. He wished Alma were window-shopping with him. An uneasy thought passed through his mind. Suppose her grandmother persuaded her not to go to California? It was like having a castle of dreams melt away. No, Alma was too willful. She did what she wanted to. He remembered that moment on the grassy slope when all at once she had reached out her hand—. Something shivery and delightful ran through him. With an effort he put that out of his mind.

He continued to the last window. A thin young man of scholarly face and a tall young woman with thick black eyebrows, hatless, had stopped in front of him to window shop. They were staring at the gloves. Bill heard her tinkle of laughter, and then they both laughed, an intimate throaty kind of laugh.

It was almost like hearing two people softly laughing from behind a bedroom door. He walked around them, but they were unaware of anyone except themselves. They were too much in love. He wondered if it would be like that someday when he really fell in love with a girl who was really in love with him. When that time came did all constraints vanish? He doubted it. He couldn't imagine Alma—he tried to shut the doors of his mind. He was only tantalizing himself by constantly thinking of Alma. Suppose she wasn't there at five o'clock? He stared through the window at what appeared to be a mechanical man of pink plastic and chromium rods, with two cameras for eyes.

The chastely printed sign in this window informed Bill that Crabtree's, Ltd., possessed the patented Photometric Robot system for taking your measurements. After selecting the material you wanted, you could have a suit fitted and ready to wear, all within fifteen minutes. Prices were forty-five and fifty-five dollars, and the Hollywood-London styled suits were seventy-five dollars and took ten minutes longer to be fitted.

While probably most of it was advertising nonsense, Bill reasoned there must be enough in it that was true to attract the steady flow of customers in and out the store. Probably that was why the Drake boys, whom Alma had known, had gone here. Too, if he could be fitted even fairly well within fifteen minutes in a forty-five dollar suit that didn't look too much like blotting paper, he'd have ample time to stop for food, to get rid of the hollow feeling before he picked up Alma's "Pink Fire" lipstick in the special container, and returned to the public library to do vigil.

So he walked into Crabtree's, Ltd.

There was a line of men waiting, about ten, several accompanied by their wives or girl friends. They were all waiting in line like people used to wait in line at the movies before television became so popular.

A dapper salesman in a regular swallow-tailed coat, striped pants, and a tie hand-painted with flowers, passed along the line, thrusting books at the men waiting in line. Bill received his book. It wasn't actually a book. Each leaf was a square section of fabric. The salesman said in a precise voice, as if he was worked by a hidden clockwork mechanism, "It will be only a short wait, sir. You'll see the price marked on each piece of cloth. The special Hollywood-London style fabrics are at the back, all carefully marked."

Bill said, "I don't know—" and he was going to say he didn't know whether he could wait quite that long. But the dapper man in the swallow-tailed coat already had moved along to someone else who had entered behind Bill. Even if Alma had recommended the place something about it made Bill feel uneasy. The light shining down from the ceiling came from long neon tubes and Bill supposed it was imitation daylight, so you could see the fabric colors as they really were. It was somehow like getting into an assembly line. A swallow-tailed clerk would dart in. A customer would dart away with him and vanish into a little cubicle. A mechanical voice from an invisible loudspeaker was explaining why the Hollywood-London styled suits at only seventy-five dollars really were cheaper in the long run for wear! For style! For class!

If he had to wait twenty-three minutes before being ushered into one of those cubicles, where he assumed the assembly line carried him through the Photometric-Robot system, even if it required only fifteen more minutes for a fitting, he didn't see where he was gaining so much time over the old-fashioned method of selecting a ready-made suit and having the tailor lengthen the trousers or sleeves.

In line directly behind Bill was the thin scholarly young man who'd looked at the display of gloves outside. The tall young woman was with him, her arm in his. She had rich dark hair cut short in that very feminine chrysanthemum-petal style which had followed the poodle-dog clip. She was dressed in a white summery frock, with darkly tanned bare legs running from the crisp line of skirt to white Mexican sandals. Bill wondered if she wasn't a little high because she didn't seem to realize anyone in front of her could hear her whispering to her thin young man. It was about some mutual joke they must have had, having to do with something she mustn't forget to buy at a drugstore if Hector honestly wanted her to help him celebrate passing his oral examination. She'd finally decided she honestly didn't care if the legless wonder was suspicious when she returned home so late tonight from her job.

The thin man whispered back, "Honestly, dear, it simply means everything to me. Why should your life be so incomplete because he had to be a hero in

Korea? But lower your voice, dear." He sounded as if he enjoyed having her whisper to him how she was going to celebrate with him, if honestly he wanted her to, before she returned home late tonight to the legless wonder, whoever the legless wonder was.

Bill disliked the soft whisperings of the couple behind him. The mechanical voice from the invisible loudspeaker continued smashing at his ears, selling the seventy-five-dollar Hollywood-London-inspired suits. Better! Finer! Classier! Perhaps he'd made a mistake not to go to one of those old-fashioned clothing stores on the other side of the street. He looked to his left for the salesman, with whom he could deposit the book of sample fabrics. When he looked to his right it surprised him to see the dapper salesman standing there, observing him.

"Here are your samples," Bill said. "I'm sorry—I can't wait longer."

The salesman ignored the book of samples. He leaned forward on his toes. Very, very lightly he touched Bill's tie with his little finger. "Ah, now, aren't you wearing one of our Fancy McMerry ties, sir? It's our very finest model, and seldom in stock. Did you buy it here?"

"No, I didn't buy it here." He remembered Alma had said she'd bought it for her brother-in-law. That must have been when she was at Drake, in Des Moines. "It was bought in Des Moines."

"In Des Moines? Really. Crabtree's hasn't a store there . . ." The voice ran down as if the clockwork had ceased ticking. "Possibly it's from an odd lot of ties, sir. You wouldn't remember where you got it in Des Moines?"

"I'm afraid not. Look. I can't wait twenty-three minutes for a fitting. I'm sorry. How do I get out of this assembly line?"

"Assembly line. That's good, *very* good, sir." The white teeth shone. "You won't have to wait a minute longer. That's why I returned to speak to you. I've very good news for you. We have this very minute completed our statistical count. What do you think? *You're* the thousandth customer to enter our portals this week! That entitles you to a free seventy-five-dollar special Hollywood-London styled suit. Just one second, sir . . ." He revolved, lifting arm and hand in an undulating motion of beckoning. "Oh, I say, Mr. Nollyfield, if you please. Mr. Nollyfield, here is our lucky customer for this week. He's wearing one of our beautiful Fancy McMerry ties, too. He bought it in Des Moines."

Mr. Nollyfield came down the aisle, beaming. He was larger than the dapper salesman and had a red carnation in his lapel. "From Des Moines?"

"Des Moines."

"And a Fancy McMerry number? What splendid taste he has, Mr. Hobart. It's nice to hear our distributor has been selling ties in Des Moines. Good for business. And I'm so pleased he's to be our lucky customer for this week."

"Look here," Bill said. "I don't want a free suit. I've got money to pay for one. But I'm short of time."

Mr. Nollyfield lifted the golden cord, permitting Bill to step away from the assembly line. "No delay, sir. We couldn't think of a thousandth customer having to pay. It would dislocate our whole good-will program. This way, please. Every thousandth customer of a Crabtree's store receives our best suit entirely free, including the Photometric-Robot's special extra ten-minute fitting. Before you can say

'Jack Robinson' you'll be walking out, sir, one of the best-dressed young men in Omaha. All free. Our compliments. Right in here, please."

Chapter Eight

Mr. Nollyfield, the plump salesman, the one with the double chins and the red carnation, ushered Bill into a gleaming cubicle filled with chromium-plated decorations, whose floor of brown cork was shaped like a large kidney. Around the curving line of floor, curving walls of pastel-tinted green rose to a glass ceiling through which shone a diffused light. Mr. Hobart had entered, shutting the door.

Bill looked around curiously. He was very much interested in how the Photometric-Robot system worked. While waiting in line, he'd seen other customers enter similar cubicles in this store. It didn't appear out of the ordinary to Bill that the Crabtree's stores offered a free seventy-five-dollar suit and fitting to every thousandth customer entering during the week. It was advertising. The TV and radio shows offered money and prizes night after night as part of their advertising programs. Movies gave you numbered stubs which would win you dishes and wrist watches and even free trips to Hollywood if your number happened to be the one the little girl drew out of the barrel every Thursday night.

So he looked around, recognizing the large photographic lamps placed like shining eyes all around the semicircular wall. Mr. Hobart had stepped behind what appeared to be a kind of camera. It was a large boxlike affair of polished metal, with a recognizable lens projecting from it.

It rested upon a tubular pedestal, apparently adjustable; the base of the pedestal was rather curious because it was fitted with four wheels set into a miniature track, like a toy-train track, that ran in a semicircle from one side of the flat wall behind Bill all around the curving wall to the other side of the flat wall. Bill now noticed, too, that lines radiated on the cork floor, in a 180 degree semicircle, toward the track.

Mr. Nollyfield was saying, "Please step against our calibrated wall graph. While we arrange the camera, you can be choosing the suiting material that most appeals to you, sir . . ." He asked the dapper man, "Mr. Hobart, where's our technician? What's detaining him?"

Behind him, Bill saw, the great flat expanse of wall from floor to ceiling was painted a light gray and covered with intersecting vertical and horizontal lines of black, something like a checkerboard. On the left side, vertically, and horizontally along the base, the lines were measured off in six-inch squares like lines on a sheet of graphing paper. It was extremely interesting. He thought he could understand the general principle of the thing. You placed yourself against the flat wall and the camera began photographing you from one vantage point and another as it was shoved along the semicircle of track. The various photographs showed your measurements blocked off in feet and inches on the squares behind you.

When Mr. Hobart began to explain, it was very much as Bill had assumed; but Mr. Hobart broke off as a door opened on the left-hand side and a short man entered in shirt sleeves, slacks, and rubber-soled shoes. Mr. Hobart promptly presented this third man as the tailoring specialist, Mr. Lenthlin, who nodded at Bill, grunting. Mr. Lenthlin didn't quite appear as Bill would have assumed a tailoring specialist for the Photometric-Robot system would appear, because in addition to being sloppily dressed he had a flat hard face and was chewing on a cigar. But he began fiddling with some of the big lights and Mr. Hobart finished explaining the general principles while Mr. Nollyfield patiently waited for Bill to select the material he wanted.

It seemed that the heart of the system was the special Polaroid camera which took twelve different photographs against the scientifically graphed background and almost immediately produced twelve completely developed positive prints. Bill nodded. He knew about Polaroid cameras. By a three-dimensional fitting chart compiled from the calibrated photographs, within less than ten minutes the experienced fitters on the assembly line downstairs had adjusted the ready-made suit most closely approximating the customer's measurements, lengthening or shortening sleeves, trousers, shoulders, and attending to all details. Time was saved by using electronic cutters as well as a plastic-cloth tape instead of old-fashioned thread. By the application of infrared rays, within four seconds the strips of plastic-cloth tape became permanently united to the suiting material and were practically invisible.

Some of it was a little confusing. Still, it sounded all right to Bill. It wasn't any more confusing than the first time he'd heard his science teacher lecture on the difference between rocket and turbo-engine propulsion. He told Mr. Nollyfield he'd like the gray gabardine, if that was available.

Mr. Nollyfield cheerfully said it so happened a fine gray gabardine was one of the numbers offered this summer in the seventy-five-dollar Hollywood-London-inspired suits.

He spoke to the man chewing the cigar. "Note that down, Mr. Lenthlin. It's our gray gabardine sports special. No mistake. This young man happens to have the very best of taste in clothes and we want him satisfied."

"Isn't that right, sir?" he asked Bill. "I saw you had the most discriminating taste as soon as our Mr. Hobart pointed out the tie you're wearing. Very few of our customers have the taste and perception to select a Fancy McMerry tie. Usually they prefer something—ah—more dull. Perhaps you're a devotee of the Mr. Future comic strip? I am, I must confess. I adore scientific progress. To let you in on a little trade secret, sir, Mr. Gramellini, our vice-president in charge of advertising, hopes to persuade the artist who draws Mr. Future to run a sequence very soon where our own Photometric-Robot system will be featured. Now, hold steady, if you please. Don't move. We're ready, Mr. Lenthlin."

Even if a great deal of it was window dressing to impress customers, still, Bill told himself if he received a gray gabardine suit that fitted him, for nothing, he had no reason to complain because he was feeling slightly foolish, backed against the big wall with the vertical and horizontal lines.

"Lights," said Mr. Hobart. Then he gave an agonized little cry. "Hold it! Mr. Nollyfield, you haven't forgotten the eyeshade?"

"By George, I nearly did," said Mr. Nollyfield and told Bill, "It's necessary to use very powerful lights for instantaneous positives, and you have to wear a small eye-shield for a minute or so. Mr. Lenthlin, where's the eye-shield?"

The man in shirt sleeves looked embarrassed. He said in a gravelly voice, "I left it downstairs."

"Well, never mind. We haven't time to get it. I'll use my handkerchief." He stepped behind Bill to tie a black silk handkerchief over Bill's eyes, but Bill jumped away. He didn't like having his eyes blindfolded.

"Now, now, sir," Mr. Nollyfield said, "It's a perfectly clean handkerchief. However—" He shrugged. "If you wish Mr. Lenthlin to go downstairs for the usual eye-shield, we can wait."

Bill had an instant of unreasoning alarm. However, everything still seemed to be on a normal level. After all, he was getting the suit for nothing. He didn't like to appear unreasonable before these three men. He'd only be blindfolded for a minute. He permitted Mr. Nollyfield to tie the folded black silk handkerchief around his eyes, and the black silk was heavier than he'd imagined a handkerchief would be and completely lightproof. Mr. Nollyfield had tied it very tightly. All at once Bill was like a blind man, and he was waiting for something to happen and at the same time trying to assure himself he was a fool to be nervous.

He felt the sudden hot shine of lights on his face. But something was wrong. The gravelly-voiced technician was saying, "He's too tall, Mr. Nollyfield. We gotta use the big camera on him."

"My dear Mr. Lenthlin, please hurry and get it, then." Mr. Nollyfield touched Bill's arm as if to reassure him and said, "It won't take but a minute longer," and Bill tried to reach up to pull the blindfold from his eyes. All at once, something hard hit the side of his head. He felt himself stagger;

next it was like being immersed in a throbbing emptiness. From very far away Mr. Nollyfield's voice assured him apologetically, "I'm frightfully sorry, letting the door hit you like that when Lenthlin swung it open." He thrust hard with his shoulder against something soft and fleshy attempting to restrain him. Perhaps he slipped. Perhaps he was shoved. He felt himself falling.

He could look upward at the imitation Old-English beams across a plaster ceiling. His eyes dully followed downward from the ceiling on one paneled oaken wall, on which were framed photographs of men in football suits, all spaced between bright pennants of Creighton U, Nebraska, Drake U, and Iowa State, at least as far as his vision extended. He was lying on what felt like a leather couch. His right arm felt numb, as if he had fallen on it.

A voice off to his left that Bill didn't recognize said quietly, "Give that scopolamine injection about five more minutes. Don't rush it."

"All right, Doc," answered a calm voice which he also failed to recognize. "Nice to have you so handy, boy. Better get back to your office."

A door slammed. The concussion of sound echoed painfully in Bill's head. He squeezed shut his eyes, trying to remember what had happened. He must have passed out. However, the scared sensation was ending. His right arm was tingling and prickling but the pain was going, and he merely felt sleepy and dull and didn't care very much what had happened:

The calm even voice Bill didn't recognize said soothingly, "You'll be quite all right again in a few minutes, boy. Lie quietly. This is our emergency rest room and lounge, available free of charge to all our customers. You hit your head on the door and then fainted. We called in Dr. Merly from next door to give you a sedative. He's assured us there's no serious damage."

When Bill turned his head toward the speaker the whole room melted together and ran like water. It came together slowly. He saw four shadowy shapes and presently distinguished Mr. Nollyfield with his red carnation, the dapper Mr. Hobart, the grubby man still chewing on the cigar, and a fourth man looking anxiously down at him. He could see the man more clearly now. Bill had an embarrassed feeling to think he'd caused them all this trouble and they'd had to call in a doctor. Whatever hypodermic the doctor had shot into his arm was beginning to give him the most wonderful sensation. His brain grew clearer each second.

The fourth man looked something like a big elephant. He was dressed in an ordinary business suit instead of a swallow-tailed coat and striped pants, and except for the impression he gave of being very big and ponderous there wasn't anything particularly unusual about him. He was about fifty or fifty-five, with a high-domed head, almost bald, small sad eyes, a big Roman nose, and a long grayish face wrinkled and creased like the hide of an elephant.

He helped Bill sit up on the couch and Mr. Nollyfield said this was Mr. Gramellini, the vice-president in charge of advertising. In his even calm voice Mr. Gramellini said could it possibly have been heat prostration? It was a stinking hot day outside. This noon, they'd had another customer faint dead away while being photographed. Those cubicles, he added, turning ponderously to the two dapper salesmen who seemed to shrink in size in comparison to him, those cubicles had better have an air-conditioning unit added. He was going to recommend air conditioning for all the photographic cubicles at the next stockholders' meeting.

Bill remembered now how scared he'd been blindfolded, thinking maybe it wasn't the door that had hit him; thinking maybe someone had pushed him. With the blindfold off everything was ordinary. A light shone through a window at the street level. He could even see legs of men and women hurrying by on the sidewalk and a few drops of rain were splashing against the window. He decided it must have been the heat and an empty stomach that had got him, after all; and he started apologizing, saying he was sorry.

But Mr. Gramellini said things like this happened. It was perfectly all right. He asked Bill to sit here quietly a few minutes longer until the sedative Dr. Merly had given wore off. The new gray gabardine suit would be ready by then, too. Bill had forgotten about that. He said he'd caused them too much trouble already. If it was all right with them, why didn't they let another customer have the suit? But, very kindly, Mr. Gramellini said he couldn't think of such a thing. He spoke briefly to Mr. Nollyfield who answered, "I'll see how much longer, Mr. Gramellini," and took himself, his double chins, and the red carnation away, the paneled oaken door shutting silently after his departure. Mr. Hobart leaned beside the wall, smiling; the man in shirt sleeves was off somewhere to the right, out of Bill's range of vision; and Mr. Gramellini sat himself ponderously upon a red leather chair with chromium legs, asking if the young gentleman cared for a cigarette while waiting. Bill said, "Yes, please."

He lighted one for Bill and one for himself, and apologetically explained he really ought to ask Bill to sign a release providing he was satisfied he had suffered no real damage. You wouldn't believe it, but there were people in this world who'd run in a minute to a shyster lawyer to sue a company for as much as they could get if they happened to trip in a store. Mr. Gramellini appeared to hesitate, his eyes gravely regarding Bill. Of course, if the young gentleman *did* believe he was more seriously injured than Dr. Merly's examination had indicated, why, then, a release shouldn't be signed. Bill felt extraordinarily dreamy and satisfied; but then he remembered Alma was going to meet him at five. When he glanced at his wrist watch he saw it was ten minutes after four.

He stood up and his legs were shaky, but they held him. He said he had to leave; he had an appointment. He'd be glad to sign anything. He repeated he was sorry he'd caused so much trouble and wondered why he was feeling so talkative. Mr. Gramellini removed a sheet of paper from a drawer in the desk, handed Bill a pen, and told Bill to read it before he signed, but it looked like a form release and Bill put his name to it. Why not? Mr. Gramellini said, "You really must give us another five minutes—" and glanced at Bill's signature, "—Mr. Evans. You can't leave without your fine new gabardine, you know."

He laughed and so did Bill, for no reason particularly except that, after all, it was very jolly and comfortable here. Mr. Gramellini asked where Bill was from and Bill told him. Mr. Gramellini began asking Bill more questions while they were waiting. Bill answered them. Bill felt better and better all the time. Except for that prickly sensation in his arm he couldn't have felt finer. He started telling Mr. Gramellini about leaving the farm early this morning to hitchhike his way to California and a couple of times, when he stopped, suddenly thinking he was talking too much to a perfect stranger, Mr. Gramellini would ask another question and off Bill would go again. He couldn't cease talking. He came to how Alma Lathrop had picked him up east of Atlantic; and by now he knew he was talking too much.

But Mr. Gramellini was so kind and so naturally interested in people that when he asked more questions Bill couldn't stop answering. Bill couldn't explain it, either. He'd recovered enough to have a part of him very much aware of sitting there, talking away while Mr. Gramellini was listening, his ponderous wrinkled face reminding Bill of a priest's face.

A part of Bill's mind harked back to the years when his father and mother had been alive and they belonged to a real church and went regularly to confession. All that had changed during the five years he'd lived with Aunt Daisy and Uncle Otis. Uncle Otis's obsession had extended against the church into which Bill had been born. He was always saying nasty, vicious things about the church Bill's parents had attended.

But all those old half-remembered feelings stirred again. It was almost like confessing to a priest even if the wholly conscious segment of Bill's mind vaguely knew it was all in reverse, somehow upside down, and Mr. Gramellini was the farthest thing possible from being a man of God.

Bill even wanted to lie but he couldn't. He had to describe Ed Murvon several times as well as the red delivery truck. It seemed that Mr. Gramellini didn't believe it. His tone of questioning got sharper. Bill felt sweat prickle under his eyelids. It *was* the truth. Mr. Gramellini sat back again. He was greatly interested in the suitcase and leather bag Alma had with her; and he was so interested he didn't bother asking Bill very much about stopping for a picnic. If he'd asked, Bill felt that he would have been compelled to tell in detail. Bill explained he'd left Alma at the Hotel St. George. She was meeting him at five o'clock at the main library in Omaha. He'd parked the Plymouth. He couldn't recall precisely where. It was eight or ten blocks from here . . .

Mr. Gramellini was standing, smiling down at him and saying, almost as a real confessor would say, "My boy, if you ask my advice, she won't meet you. Those flashy yellow-haired girls come a dime a dozen, my boy. She picked you up. You amused her for an hour or so, but she won't really meet you. She was only making sport of you, my boy."

Bill tried to say Alma wasn't a flashy yellow-haired girl. He couldn't remember describing Alma to have given Mr. Gramellini such an impression of her. But Mr. Nollyfield had returned, carrying the new gray gabardine suit. Everything began going faster and faster.

Bill was ushered inside a small dressing room where he hastily changed, not forgetting to transfer his wallet from his old pair of trousers to the new. His free outfit consisted only of coat and trousers. The coat was too tight across the shoulders, the sleeves were an inch too short, and the trousers kept riding up on his ankles. But when he stepped back into the lounge Mr. Hobart cried delightedly, "Perfect! Perfect!" although by now Bill knew it wasn't at all perfect.

He was still feeling confused. But where for a time he had felt as if he had been strangely deprived of any will to independent action, now a resistance was gathering in him against these clothing-store gentlemen. Somehow they had taken him in, he felt. If this was an advertising program to increase business, it was a damned lousy program. The new suit fitted badly. Still, there was no use beefing. He had received it all for free. All right.

They were tugging here and there at his coat, Mr. Nollyfield and Mr. Hobart exclaiming delightedly. Bill wrenched away to look at his watch. Five minutes to five! He had to get out of here. Someone shoved an untidy parcel into his hands, carelessly wrapped. It was his old windbreaker and corduroys. There was one thing more. His tie. It wasn't right for a gray gabardine. Mr. Nollyfield had a new tie for him, a nice gray silk tie, all free. Now, without as much as a by-your-leave, the grubby man in shirt sleeves got in front of Bill, puffing stale cigar smoke in Bill's face, reaching to remove Bill's tie.

Everything broke in Bill's mind, like a log jam coming loose. They'd been having a game with him, he decided. He was the country boy fresh from the sticks. That was what it was, these four men ganging up and amusing themselves on a hot sticky afternoon. Bill stuck his hand flat against the man's chest and pushed. He had the whiplash muscles a young man starts having along about sixteen and retains until twenty-five or twenty-six, before the resiliency and spring-steel quality slowly starts rusting off a little each year. Bill hadn't realized he'd pushed so hard and furiously.

The man's flat head snapped back, the soggy cigar flew away from the yellow teeth; and there was the sound of something crashing against the door. Instantly, the man started back at Bill, but Mr. Gramellini said, "Hold it," in a way Bill hadn't heard him speak before. And the man in shirt sleeves held it.

That was all there was to it.

Bill didn't know what had possessed him. Everything became ordinary and commonplace. Mr. Gramellini was saying severely Mr. Lenthlin should know better than to puff cigar smoke in a customer's face. It was outrageous. Little cries of agreement came from both Mr. Hobart and Mr. Nollyfield.

Bill removed the tie. He accepted the new one from Mr. Gramellini, even thanking him, and tied it in front of a mirror whose reflection showed the flat eyes of the man in shirt sleeves staring at him not with hatred but with something grinning in them.

Mr. Gramellini opened the door. In that grave kindly voice of an older man trying to be helpful to a young man having to make his own way he said, "If I were you, Mr. Evans, I should forget the chance meeting you had on the road with a young lady who, by all standards, does seem rather unpredictable. We have quite a few Creighton U college boys as steady customers. From what they tell me, I can assure you it's become quite the thing, you might say, among certain classes of young women to pick up hitchhikers along the road and pretend to fall in love with them and agree to go a great distance. It's rather brutal, really. I suppose it's a game with them like driving hot rods hands off. But don't be taken in. Take my advice. Get on to your destination, sir. In the name of Crabtree's Limited, let me thank you for your valued patronage and congratulate you on winning such a beautiful gray gabardine. Good day, sir. Mr. Nollyfield, show him to the side door, please."

Mr. Nollyfield pulled at Bill's arm, leading him to the left, past a long wooden table on which were heaped piles of dingy-looking men's slacks with a sign on the table saying: "Crabtree's Bargain Basement. Prices 50% Off This Week!" When they came to a door Mr. Nollyfield let go of Bill, opened it, and said, "O.K., get going, boy," with nothing at all any more of that bright cheerful subservient way of speaking.

Bill walked up a flight of cement steps, finding himself on the sidewalk. It was beginning to rain. It was past five o'clock. He headed in the direction of the park, with a feeling of having escaped by the skin of his teeth. But he didn't know what it was he'd escaped. He clutched his paper package, walking very fast. It was only a few minutes after five. Alma had said she might be a little late but he wasn't to worry. He wasn't to rush himself, either. If she arrived first, she would wait.

It was growing dark from the approaching storm and he wasn't quite certain where the drugstore was. He didn't want to forget the present he'd bought for Alma.

There was still a kind of ringing in his ears. Automobiles were snarling and honking horns, in a hurry to get home before the summer storm broke. Far off, thunder sounded high above the city. Suppose Alma didn't meet him? Suppose it was as Mr. Gramellini had said, a cruel joke girls liked to play on hitchhikers? But Mr. Gramellini had Alma all wrong. She'd be there.

He knew what it was now that gave him a feeling of something still crawling uncleanly on his flesh. It was as if he'd been somewhere where candles were burning all the wrong way, with an altar covered with obscenities, where that ponderous man with the wrinkled face was acting as a confessor—but not as a man of God. He saw the drugstore at the other end of the block, and he ran, with rain falling in great drops out of the darkening sky.

Chapter Nine

Probably because it was so close to closing time, no customers were waiting at the cosmetic counter. The girl with the friendly pug face was busy counting her sales stubs. She remembered him right away. She had his gift ready, wrapped in a crinkly silver-cellophane paper. She said, "I'd almost given you up—" and regarded him with unabashed curiosity. "You weren't wearing *that* suit, were you, this afternoon?"

"No. I got a new suit at Crabtree's." He looked down at his trousers. They appeared sleazy after being wet by the rain. "It's a rotten fit, isn't it? I walked into Crabtree's and I expect I was taken. But I got it free. It was one of those advertising deals."

She said sympathetically he ought to have gone to Martin and Somerlane's. They had good men's clothes. By now almost everyone in Omaha knew Crabtree's was owned by Sid Gramellini. Last month the grand jury had tried to indict him, but failed for lack of proof that he ran the vice racket here. Gramellini was supposed to use his store as a front like that racketeer on the west coast had used a haberdashery store. Because prices were dirt cheap and they advertised that Photometric-Robot thing, they did a big business; but none of the men she knew ever bought clothes there.

She smiled. "Anyway, you didn't pay for it. I suppose you've got a date now with your girl to give her that fancy lipstick job?"

Alma wasn't really his girl but something warm and exciting touched his mind just to think of seeing her in a few more minutes. He said, "If I don't get washed away," stuck the gift in his pocket, and shoved the parcel of his old clothes under his arm. She said, "Here," impulsively, reaching under the counter for an umbrella. It was an old one, she said. It had been kicking around for ages. He could take it. He wouldn't have to bother to return it.

He hurried through the park. By now, rain was pouring. Even if the umbrella had been kicking around for ages it shed most of the water. That pug-faced girl had been unexpectedly kind. Having her give him the umbrella helped balance his experience in the clothing store. He wouldn't tell Alma he had walked into a place owned by a racketeer. Even if he was so fresh from the country that that girl behind the cosmetic counter had been able to guess where he was from, he wasn't going to let Alma know exactly how easily he'd been taken in.

On the corner below the park he waited impatiently for the green light. Through the rain the gray bulk of the library building dimly loomed before him on the other side of the street. A crowd of forty or fifty people was milling around the opposite corner. It looked as if there had been an accident. His heart gave a great thump of agony. Not Alma? He didn't wait for the light to change. He chased around in front of a truck whose horn bellowed at him. An ambulance was there. A cop in a streaming slicker shouted, "Break it up!" Two white-coated men from the ambulance were lifting a slack body from wet concrete.

Bill had a glimpse of wet yellow hair. He thought it was Alma. She'd been waiting for him. An automobile must have swerved on the wet asphalt when turning the corner, to run up over the curb and smash into her. Bill moved forward, violently. No, it wasn't Alma. The men were shoving the body into the rear of the ambulance, the head flopping loosely. Rain had washed away the blood. It was that brassy-haired girl in the green jacket and skirt who had been an hour and a half early for whoever she was waiting for. The ambulance doors slammed shut.

Someone near Bill said, "She's dead. Damn those hot rod kids and the way they drive! Why doesn't the city do something?"

Bill slowly climbed the library steps. His legs were shaky. For that instant when he had thought it was Alma he had felt all his spirit go out of him. He wouldn't have believed a girl could mean that much to him when he had known her for less than half a day. She wasn't his girl. She never could be. He was still more than eighteen hundred miles away from his destination, surrounded by a strange city. The ambulance departed. The crowd was breaking up. Bill looked around for Alma. She ought to be here any minute.

He couldn't help thinking of that brassy-haired girl who had been waiting, and waiting, too, for someone. Now she would never know whether the fellow for whom she'd been waiting ever came or not. Something all at once seemed to open and close in Bill's head. This was the second blonde girl whom he'd seen in trouble today. This one—the brassy-haired girl—was now miserably dead. But there had been that thin lemon-haired blonde back in that crumby grocery store. That screwball had almost shot her.

Bill had the most extraordinary impression. It was as if that door in his mind was trying to swing open wider, instead of closing, for him to sight more clearly what was there. Two blondes. Alma was also a blonde, though her hair was a soft, more natural color. One had been almost shot. A second had been mangled horribly. Both times, too, Alma had been in the area—at least, she should have been here at the library, tonight, at five. He felt a shivery coldness. He was nuts! He put it out of his head. What he needed was food. Everything was getting more and more fantastic. He was going off his rocker. Where was Alma? My God, she couldn't have stood him up, could she?

He waited. He waited until it was twenty-five long minutes after five. She should have been here long before now. Automobile lights flashed in the rain. Bill edged closer to one of the bronze library doors. What was delaying her? Now it was six o'clock. She had promised to be here at five or not much after. She had to come. How pretty she was! He could almost believe he had fallen a little in love with her. Why didn't she get here? Perhaps she wasn't coming. Perhaps she had never intended to meet him at five or at any other time. Something began shriveling inside him.

He waited until fifteen minutes after six; but did not completely give up all hope. He crossed to the other side of the street and entered a combined cigar store and short-order restaurant. He sat at the end of the counter where he could watch the library. He refused to believe she had tricked him.

He ordered buttermilk and two hamburgers with all the trimmings. The waitress serving the order had seen the accident across the street. She was full of it, ready to talk to anyone. "I was standin' right here," she said, "an' jus' lookin' across the street. I noticed her there 'cause she'd been there maybe a coupla hours yet, jus' waitin'. This big car stopped anna fella gets out. I think to myself 'well it's about time,' thinkin' it was her fella. But the fella jus' grabs her suitcase. She starts yellin'. I keep a lookin'. The fella runs to the car. He pushes her. He jumps in, drives it right into her and keeps goin', and alla time I was lookin'. Nobody did nothin'. Everybody jus' looked when she was smashed."

Bill wished she'd please shut up and take herself to the other end of the counter. He was hungry and had that hollow feeling but there wasn't much meat in the sandwiches. They were filled mostly with relish. He left a half-finished sandwich on the plate. He went to the pay telephone booth, deciding to call the Hotel St George. What was Alma's grandmother's name? Mrs. Ralph Lathrop.

Over the wire a voice said nobody by the name of Mrs. Ralph Lathrop was registered here and hung up. He went through the business of dropping more coins in the slot. The same voice said the same thing, more sharply; but before it could hang up he asked desperately if a Miss Alma Lathrop wasn't registered, either . . .

It was like having the bottom drop out of all his world. She had never intended to go to California with him. She had sent him off to Omaha in that rented car as an excuse to get rid of him. She'd seen the name of the Hotel St. George on that billboard they had passed before entering Council Bluffs, had him drive to the hotel, had entered, had probably remained only long enough in the lobby for him to drive off before going to wherever her grandmother really lived.

But Bill had the hundred and fifty dollars she had shoved into his hands. That was too much. It didn't make sense. He halted at the cash register to pay for the two hamburgers and the buttermilk. She might have given him five or ten dollars when shoving him off, as a sop to her conscience; but here he was with a hundred and fifty dollars. It was more than enough to buy a bus ticket to California. It didn't make any sense at all.

He wanted to sit down somewhere to reason it out. What was he to do? He stopped for a moment in the doorway, looking out upon the shining black street, people hurrying in the rain, car tires screeching, lights shining wetly. One of those small English cars was crawling along in the traffic, going west past the doorway and stopping at the corner, waiting until the slow red light changed to green.

Bill started up; that was Alma driving the car! She didn't see him. She was peering through her left-hand window toward the library on the opposite side of the street. Bill ran. Lights changed to green. People on the sidewalk blocked his way. The little English car darted around a bigger American car, turned right, and was gone.

Was it Alma? What would she be doing in an English car? Bill muttered, "'Scuse me," when he bumped into someone. He backed under a doorway. If it was Alma she might drive around the block for a second look at the library steps. Bill didn't know how long he waited there by the library.

Rain sluiced along the street. Perhaps he had waited ten minutes when all at once again he saw the little Hillman Minx. This time it was approaching slowly despite the raucous honks from a traffic line behind it.

He dropped the umbrella and ran from the doorway into the street. It was Alma. He shouted, "Alma! Alma!" rapping on the window.

Startled, she looked in his direction. She was so surprised she stalled the engine. Hastily she opened the door.

"My gosh, am I glad to see you!" she said. "We'll find a gas station somewhere and see how we get out of town."

He had found her. She was unharmed. Nothing had happened to her except that she was driving this little car. All his concern had been for nothing. Here she was; he had wanted to get back to her more than anything else in the world. He looked at her, seeing her only dimly in the darkness inside the little car. She had lied to him about her grandmother. Why had she? he was thinking numbly. There was something terribly wrong and he knew it, and also he knew that he did not really want to know. But he had to know.

Chapter Ten

He sat in the seat and said, "Where'd you get the car?"

"Like it? At a second-hand dealer's near Granny's, it's why I've been so long."

He wanted so very much to believe her.

"What about the Plymouth? I left it parked."

"Oh, that?" She was taking it casually enough. "I thought I told you the Plymouth belonged to Granny. She decided I'd better not drive it to California, after all. You've got the parking check, haven't you?" she asked carelessly. "I'll mail the parking check to Granny and she can have the man bring the car around to her. She won't be in any hurry. She never liked it much, anyway. That's why she let me use it at Drake."

"I left my knapsack in the Plymouth," he heard himself saying. He had either gone insane and had never twice phoned that hotel, or Alma's soft clear voice was lying horribly. She did not sound as if she was lying.

"Do we have to waste time going back for your knapsack, honey? I've had an awful afternoon, arguing with Granny and phoning clear to California to tell Sis I was coming and—and buying this heap in a hurry. Now all I want to do is to keep on going. Look. There's a gas station. We'll fill up. Then I wish you would drive for awhile."

After they had traded places at the gasoline station, she said, "You haven't noticed my hair."

Enough light was shining through the windows from the gas station for him to see her more clearly. Her hair was cut short, but not too short. It had been cut with an engaging unevenness, like a clustering of chrysanthemum petals. She'd changed into a sleeveless linen dress. Her legs were bare and she was wearing sandals. Instead of a girl of twenty-two, you could almost believe she was a girl of just sixteen going for a ride with Bill on a warm rainy evening in June.

He pulled away from the station, going two blocks to the north where he could turn right to enter the boulevard leading west out of the city to the big highway. She asked, "Don't you like my hair?" He didn't know. His stomach was cramping. Why had she lied to him? He said he thought it made her look younger. He heard her soft laugh. It was why she'd had it cut. She hadn't wanted to look like an old hag of twenty-two while driving across the continent with him.

She asked him why he'd ever selected *that* suit? She didn't want to hurt his feelings; but—honestly! She'd had a chance to look at him under the lights of that gas station. The suit didn't even fit him. He explained how he had received it free as part of an advertising campaign run by Crabtree's.

"My heavens," she said. "I don't know how you could have let them fit you with such an awful suit. I wish I hadn't told you to go there. I thought it was a good store."

He didn't tell her he had heard it was owned by a Sid Gramellini who was supposed to be a racketeer. He skipped most of the other details, too. The little Hillman charged along easily. They were passing through the suburbs, into the country. He could smell the fresh wet smell of newly plowed fields somewhere off in the blackness.

"Bill," she said, "we'll buy you a decent outfit Monday. If you need more money—"

"No. I'm going to give you back your money. I've enough of my own to keep me going to Sacramento."

"Now, Bill. We talked that all over this afternoon."

"I want to ask you a question."

"Yes?"

"It's none of my business. You don't have to answer. Are you in some sort of trouble? Are you running away from something?"

"Geez, why should I be running away?"

"You don't have to tell me if you don't want to."

Her voice became thin. "What's all this about? Let's have it. Go on."

"I started thinking after I phoned the hotel."

"What hotel?"

"The Hotel St. George. I phoned twice. No one by the name of Mrs. Ralph Lathrop was registered there. That's your grandmother's name, isn't it?"

"Of course she's registered there. I don't understand."

"All right," Bill said. "I just asked."

"No, let's get it settled. We can't go on like this if you think I'm lying to you. Why should I be running away from anything? Gracious! I've finished school. I'm in a hurry to get back to California. Yes, I suppose I'm tired of Iowa and the Middle West. Maybe I am running away and wanting to get back to Sis. But what's wrong about that? I just can't understand why you phoned Granny."

"I thought you weren't going to meet me. I didn't know how to reach you except by phoning your grandmother."

"Listen, honey. I didn't mean to keep you waiting. I'm sorry. But Granny was there all afternoon. For the past two years she's had Apartment Six in the residential annex of the Hotel St. George. If you phoned the annex and asked for her—"

"The *annex?*"

"Oh, Bill! You phoned the hotel, not the annex?"

She began laughing. All at once everything was warm and friendly again, even better than it was this afternoon. His bones ached. He was nearly pooped. But here he was, with Alma beside him. The little Hillman ran along at fifty-five miles an hour like a charm through the warm summer rain. Iowa was behind them. Omaha was behind them. He'd been nearly out of his head for a little while, believing she'd dumped him. He wanted to apologize for thinking she had been lying to him.

She placed her hand over his hand. "Let's just stop kicking each other around and enjoy ourselves. Doesn't the air smell good? I hope it rains all night. I'm getting kinda hungry, though. Suppose we stop to eat pretty soon."

At eight-thirty they stopped for dinner in a town like any of the other little Nebraska towns they had passed through. Not many people were eating at this hour. They had a booth in a far corner. The waitress said the steaks were good. That was what they both ordered, rare steaks, French fries, and salad. Alma said if it was all the same to Bill, she wanted milk. Bill ordered beer. While they waited he picked up a folded copy of a newspaper left on the seat in the booth.

It was an early-afternoon edition of the Lincoln, Nebraska, *Journal*. On the front page it had a smeared two-column cut of a stocky man going into what looked like a courtroom. He had one arm flung over his face, to hide it from the newspaper photographer. Underneath the caption it said it was a wirephoto of a photograph of Monk Anzeiger, taken last year in Milwaukee when he had been questioned by the district attorney in regard to a holdup. This was the man who was wanted for the armored-truck robbery at Boone, Iowa, early this morning. Six hundred thousand dollars had been removed from the smashed truck during the daring attack. Bill stared at that newspaper photograph. He tried to recall the photograph of Monk Anzeiger printed in the Omaha newspaper and only remembered a square heavy face with eyes blurred by glasses. Because of the arm hiding the face in this one, here, it wasn't much of a photograph to identify anyone. However, there was something about the attitude of the man, and the square stocky body, which all at once put him in mind of Ed Murvon. He felt the oddest sort of tingling. He had almost forgotten Ed Murvon in that souped-up red Dodge delivery truck. Alma's shoulder pressed Bill's as she leaned forward to see the newspaper headlines.

"Six hundred thousand dollars?" she exclaimed. "But that *can't* be!"

He'd forgotten that probably she'd been so rushed this afternoon she hadn't yet had time to read about the armored-truck robbery. The overhead neon lights gave her face a greenish hue.

"Six hundred thousand dollars?" she repeated. "It just can't be. There's a frame in. They've framed it."

Bill said hell, no, the newspaper claimed it was all Federal reserve money. It looked like the real thing. How could it be framed? That was why all the roads had been blocked this morning toward

Council Bluffs. There had even been a police check at the bridge. She didn't answer.

The waitress arrived with the tray. Before starting to eat Bill folded the *Journal* and stuck it in his coat pocket. He wanted to look at that photograph when he had more time. A reward of five thousand dollars was offered for any information leading to the capture of Monk Anzeiger and the recovery of the stolen money.

Alma wasn't very hungry, but Bill was ravenous. As he ate he wondered how you could get rid of six hundred thousand dollars in bank notes. It would be a pile of money. Probably it would fill a small trunk. Again he seemed to see the red delivery wagon with the sign on the panels saying: *Old Farm Brand Coffee & Spices*. That engine had been souped up. It hadn't been an ordinary engine. Ed's eyes had been like little pebbles, too, when he had caught Bill looking into the empty delivery truck and seeing only a bedroll and a forty-five gun in a shabby holster. In a truck like that, you could carry a trunk filled with six hundred thousand dollars. No one would think anything about it.

Bill finished his steak and salad, beginning to get back almost to being himself again. His mind continued reaching out. If you had a coffee and spice truck, you wouldn't need a trunk. You could use a wooden case which had been filled with coffee cans. Why not? Perhaps your job was to pick up the money from the hoodlums who'd actually shot up the truck and get the money out of the state. You'd have a couple of hours leeway in that delivery truck before a search could be organized and all the roads blocked.

It would be enough. The case would be marked "Old Farm Brand Coffee." All you had to do was stop at one of the little towns on the Rock Island line and give the case to the express agent. You could explain you were sending a shipment to a customer in Chicago or New York. For that matter, you wouldn't even have to explain. It would be merely another routine shipment for the express agent. Well, why not? Perhaps it was screwy; but it seemed to Bill that there was a connection, after all. He drank the last of his beer and turned excitedly to Alma.

"Remember I told you I hitched a ride with that man in the red delivery truck? That when I happened to look inside, it didn't have any cans of coffee or spices in it? He was stockily built, like the man in the newspaper photograph. Do you suppose he had something to do with that armored truck thing this morning? Maybe I'm nuts. But I can see how he could get rid of the money—"

"Bill," she said, "for God's sake, don't be a kid. Let's not play cops and robbers. I don't want a dessert. I had a snack at Granny's. Do you want something more?"

He shook his head. No, he'd had all he wanted. She couldn't have said anything more withering than saying crossly, "Let's not play cops and robbers." Bill stopped thinking about Ed Murvon and how Ed Murvon might safely get rid of all that money. The waitress placed a bill for four dollars and twenty cents on the table and Bill paid it with money from his wallet. After the waitress had gone, he tried to give Alma back her hundred and fifty dollars. Even more crossly she said would he please stop worrying about that money? They'd agreed it would be a loan, hadn't they? They could settle how much he owed her when they arrived in

Sacramento. He was to keep the money and do the paying on the way.

He wished he was twenty-five and was the one who was taking Alma to California, not the other way around. For a couple of seconds, Bill and Alma just sat there. Finally, Bill said, "I bought you a present in Omaha," and that sounded wrong, too. He pulled the little square package from his damp coat pocket. It didn't look like very much. The crinkly silver-cellophane wrapping was all crushed. He noticed now she was wearing lipstick. She must have bought herself a lipstick in Council Bluffs. He said he'd bought it with his own money and that sounded even more wrong.

She gave Bill a funny look. He heard the rain beating at the restaurant windows. He had gone a long way tonight, much longer than he'd ever thought he'd go. "Bill," she said, "it's lovely. You shouldn't have." She wasn't sore any more. Before leaving she even wiped off her own lipstick with the paper napkin, opened her purse to look at herself in the little mirror, and used the lipstick he'd bought her to make up her lips again. He liked watching her. She'd never looked so beautiful. She squeezed his hand. "I'm going to start falling for you if I don't be careful." He knew she was joking, of course. But he was glad he'd remembered to buy her the lipstick, "Pink Fire" shade. On the way out he dropped the folded copy of the *Journal* on the counter. He didn't want it. He wasn't playing cops and robbers.

There was another moment, too, after they'd dashed through the rain into the sanctuary of the little English car. Before he could switch on the lights her voice said, "After fixing my lips for you I can't really kiss you without smearing you. It'll have to be a little feather kiss. Don't move . . ." She held his face between her hands. She touched his lips lightly at first, and then they both stopped caring whether or not her lipstick smeared.

Afterward she gave him a piece of tissue from her bag to wipe his mouth. She said shakily, "Bill, we're crazy. I'm four years older than you. We can't ever start kissing each other like that again. I never meant—"

"I'm falling in love with you. You might as well know."

"But, Bill, we only met this morning! If you ever say anything that silly again you'll have to leave me and start walking. Now let's get going. I like driving at night."

She huddled on her side, as far away from him as possible. Perhaps she slept for a time; he didn't know. The little Hillman pursued an endless road. As he drove on and on the strangest fancy came to him. While he knew it wasn't true, it was as if Alma and he were both fleeing from something following after them like a great black dog. Even though he was young with all the reserves of youth, by ten that night he had reached his limit. He would find himself falling asleep at the wheel. His head would jerk up. He had to tell Alma he couldn't hang on much longer.

She roused herself. Her voice sounded small and rueful. "I'm awfully selfish. I was half asleep. Stop at the first place you see."

A mile later he saw a vacancy sign gleaming dimly in the rain. He turned into a gravel lane, stopping at the first cottage. He didn't know how near the motel court was to the next town and was too nearly dead on his feet to care. They must have driven a hundred miles since leaving Omaha. He pushed a bell, waited, and pushed again.

The woman who opened the door had thrown a purple dressing gown on over a cotton nightgown. Her stringy hair was in metal curlers. He said his sister and he wanted rooms for the night. The woman's lips compressed. Bill was afraid she was going to refuse him when Alma called sleepily, "Bill, take anything available. I'll fall asleep in two minutes."

The lights from the cottage shone on her blonde hair and her face. The woman looked at her and back to Bill. She said apologetically, "I guess you are brother and sister at that. She's got your eyes and color hair, all right. I try to run a respectable place. Sometimes young couples—" She didn't finish what she was going to say concerning young couples.

The cottage she gave them had one big bedroom with a door to the bathroom, and a smaller bedroom at the side. After Bill carried in Alma's neat canvas suitcase he assumed she would want the big bedroom. But she shook her head; it was too near the front door. He could sleep in here and protect her if anyone tried to sneak in. She grinned, making a joke of it. But she shut the door of the small bedroom behind her.

He missed the pajamas in his knapsack. He was going to have to sleep raw. Through her door Alma called, asking if he'd please run hot water in the tub for her to take a quick bath. If there was a tub.

There was. He got the water running, hastily shucked himself out of his damp clothes, switched off the light, and slid under a damp sheet, pulling the thin blanket over the sheet. A little later Alma rapped on her door. Could she pass through? It was all right, he answered.

She wasn't very long with her bath. It was less than fifteen minutes. She stopped for a moment by his bed. She looked small and shadowy. She had turned the water on for his bath, she said. She hoped she hadn't taken too long. She bent her face down to him. "Good night, Bill. I do like you very much and I haven't any lipstick on now." Her lips brushed his, lightly. He reached for her. But if was as if he had run all day until he had nothing left in him; and now he tried to spur himself for another run. He felt silk slide through his fingers. Her soft laugh was faintly sympathetic, but her door closed firmly.

In the tub he nearly fell asleep. Perversely, he could not sleep when he returned to the strange bed. Because his mind was too tightly wound up, it would not unwind and relax. It kept going back and back to everything that had happened to him today. If he had had only a series of random encounters, it meant nothing at all. If all was coincidence it was of no use to beat his brains out trying to find a meaning. In review isolated scenes passed across his mind, of himself meeting one person after another: Ed Murvon, Alma, that lemon-haired girl in the grocery store, back to Alma, Council Bluffs, that friendly girl in the cosmetics department, the brassy-haired girl on the library steps—the girl who had been so horribly mangled, the men at Crabtree's, back toward the library, finding that that girl with brassy hair was the one run over, not Alma as at first he had thought. He could not forget those two blonde girls, one who had been nearly shot, the other run over, done dead as hell. What was it? He felt fear touch at him.

His mind moved forward in time along the hours of this afternoon. Again he was standing in front of the clothing store which Alma had recommended because Drake boys, she knew, who lived in Omaha, went there. He was going to buy a new suit for himself. But he had paused to sight into that window with the display of hand-painted ties. He had been wearing a Crabtree number, too, evidently a very special number. Afterward, Gramellini or one of the salesmen had persuaded him to remove the Fancy McMerry tie and accept one of plain silk. But what could be a connection between blonde girls and a tie and everything else? It seemed to him a meaning was waiting for him just beyond the outer edge of consciousness, but he was too bushed to think that far.

A dog was whining from outside in the wet darkness. Gradually, the whining sound distracted him. He sat upright in bed. It was a small and rather horrible whining. When he listened he was not even sure he was hearing it. He could imagine a little black dog making that sound. It would be sick and hungry and crouching near the door, whining to be let in.

When he got up and opened the door he could see nothing at all. Rain splattered on his naked skin. He shut the front door. He was cautiously feeling his way in the darkness to his bed when again he heard the whining; he stopped. It came from Alma's bedroom. She hadn't latched the inner door. He opened it, listening. She was crying in her sleep. It was like listening to the whining of a little black dog. The sound made his flesh crawl.

Chapter Eleven

Sunday morning couldn't have been better. The air was bright and all the rain had ended. While Alma finished dressing, Bill checked oil and gas and the tires and had a few minutes to look at the road map. The quickest way to the coast was through Cheyenne. It was less than four hundred miles away. By tomorrow night they should be in Salt Lake City, Tuesday night, somewhere near Reno; and with any luck, that would put Bill in Sacramento sometime Wednesday afternoon.

They had breakfast at the next town. But they were on the road again by nine-thirty. Sometimes when passing through the little Nebraska towns they heard the sound of church bells and once through green trees they saw people in their best clothes gathered around a white church.

The hot morning sun had dried the highway. Bill had changed back into his corduroys and had tossed that sleazy gabardine suit into the rear of the car. It was too tight. He never wanted to wear it again. This was the second day he was wearing the woolen shirt, the shorts and the socks, but he would have to do with them until tomorrow when the stores opened. He needed a shave, too. Before evening he'd have to remember to stop at a drug store for a razor, a toothbrush, and such.

It became warmer. Alma was wearing the linen dress she had bought yesterday afternoon. It still looked fresh and new on her and she had lazied back on her side of the seat while the miles flung themselves by. She had kicked off her sandals, with her bare legs running down to the floor mat.

In the bright Nebraska sunlight everything was different than it was last night when Bill had imagined a black dog was whining. Suppose Alma had been disturbed in her sleep by an unpleasant dream? She wasn't the first girl or the last to cry softly for a few minutes in her sleep before sinking into a deeper sleep.

While they were driving along that morning they started talking about what Bill was going to do when he reached Sacramento. How certain was Bill of getting a job on the newspaper? While he couldn't say until he got there, Bill believed Mr. Pearson would probably do all he could for him. Mr. Pearson was the editor of the *Star*. Bill's mother had been his secretary.

Alma asked if Bill had heard from Mr. Pearson—did Bill know he was still there? He was, Bill knew that. At least twice a year Bill would get a letter from him, asking how Bill was doing. The last one had come only two months ago. Mr. Pearson had thought a lot of Bill's father. Bill's father had worked on a Cedar Rapids newspaper before resigning to go into the Air Force. Bill had been seven when his father had won a Pulitzer prize for his editorials. At the time he had been too young to know how much a Pulitzer prize meant. Later he had learned newspapermen all over the country had heard about William Evans. Bill hoped someday he could be as good as his father had been.

"What's the Pulitzer prize?" Alma asked out of a clear sky.

She'd graduated from Drake U. Drake had a first-rate journalism school. When Bill glanced at her he didn't know what sort of an astonished expression was on his face; but she recovered very quickly. She patted his knee. "Don't look like that. Can't a girl tease you?"

They had had a late breakfast so they continued driving through the noon hour. They came into the town of Ogalla about one-thirty. Here the highway forked. The main highway ran west to Cheyenne, one hundred and sixty miles away; and a secondary paved highway swung off through hills toward Denver, two hundred and fifteen miles to the southwest. Bill wanted to go straight on to Cheyenne. That was the shorter road to Salt Lake City.

Alma said vexedly, "Damn! We've got to go through Denver. When I was in Council Bluffs I thought we passed through Denver. Granny wanted me to take some presents to my sister. I was in too much of a rush to meet you to wait for Granny to pack them. I promised to pick them up at Denver if she could get them mailed on the night train."

He silently studied the road sign. Presently Bill asked why her grandmother hadn't mailed the presents to Alma's sister in San Francisco? Wouldn't it have been easier? She turned her head to him. She was slim and cool and a little remote. She could have been speaking to a boy of ten who was making a nuisance of himself.

"My sister happens to be married, Mr. Curiosity. She happens to be expecting a baby in a couple of months. Instead of dropping in on her empty-handed, it might be better if I walked in with some of the things Granny's been knitting like mad. Are you satisfied? Suppose we see if we can eat here. I'm hungry."

It was a drowsy town, that Sunday, located where the Nebraska prairies began rising toward the blue line of mountains along the bright horizon. The place in which they ate was a cattle-town catch-all. On the left hand side was a soda fountain and a short-order lunch counter. Their orders were taken by a brisk young person in faded jeans and red and white checked cotton shirt. She was wearing a gold cross at her throat and appeared pleasantly serene for such a hot afternoon. Bill surmised she had been to church this morning.

After eating, Bill told Alma he'd better try to buy a razor and stuff while he had the chance. Hardware, grain, and feed were in the middle of the store. Drugs and sundries were on the other side. The stooped gray man, who evidently was the father of the young person in jeans, was somewhere in the rear. With him were two men dressed in stiff Sunday clothes and wearing Stetsons. Western, saddles hung from the ceiling. A small tractor was even there, dimly perceived through the hot dusty air.

The brisk young person in jeans had promptly transferred herself to the drugs and sundries counter. He bought razor, soap, toothbrush, and a comb. She dropped them in a sturdy Manila bag. From behind him he heard Alma's soft clear voice engaged in conversation with a man's deeper voice. He looked over his shoulder. A tall fellow was casually resting an elbow on the lunch counter. The face was tanned the color of saddle leather. They were discussing last night's rain. It was shore good for feed grass, Miss. Yes, Alma said, smiling up at the lean tanned face; but all that rain hadn't been very pleasant for her brother and herself driving in it last night.

The young person briskly asked Bill, "What else?"

He swung his head back to the drugs and notions counter. He paused a second. Alma had told him she hoped it would rain all night. She'd acted like she'd enjoyed driving in the rain with him. He hadn't been just the kid brother then.

"Nothing else?"

"Yes," Bill said. "Have you a small notebook, please?"

That she did, for ten cents. He wanted one to keep a record of every cent he spent for himself on the trip. At the end of the trip he could total up accurately how much he owed Alma. While the brisk young person briskly added his purchases, Bill idly noticed a rack filled with picture magazines. All had gaudy covers, usually of sensational-looking young women. One cover in particular caught his eye. On the stand next to the magazines he noticed a display of paper-covered books, reprints and originals.

But Bill wasn't interested in buying any of the books; he was too wrathfully interested in the conversation that tall young rancher was having with Alma. *It shore was fine weather today, Miss.* Bill felt stabbed by jealousy.

Bill wondered even more wrathfully if he was supposed to wait here until Alma decided to terminate such an interesting conversation about the weather. It was all right with him if that was what Alma wanted. Rather blindly he reached for one of the paper-bound books on the rack. He had drawn a thirty-five cent dictionary. He opened it for Alma to see, if she cared, that he was completely engrossed. It was nothing to him if she wanted to waste her time with the first cowboy she met. Pages leafed open in his hand and his eyes saw *scopulous scopus, scorbutic.* Then all at once he started searching frantically, but the word he was searching for was not listed.

The young person in jeans came through to him by informing him it was a very good dictionary, actually, for only thirty-five cents. He said, "It doesn't have the word I wanted."

"Perhaps I can help? I'm getting pretty good at words. I'm going to try for that five-hundred-dollar prize on the 'Guess What' radio show every Sunday night from Omaha. Haven't you heard it?"

He shook his head. Alma had glanced at him, giving him an apologetic smile as if only now she realized he was waiting for her. She arose and passed through the doors to the porch and out into the dusty sunshine. The tall cowboy strolled along with her. Bill went to the entrance; he heard the cowboy saying that was shore a purty little car, Miss.

He had not noticed that the young person in jeans was still with him until she said cheerfully, "You know, I've been after Pa to buy me one of those English cars. What's yours, an Austin?"

"No, a Hillman Minx . . ."

He had moved toward the steps. But the young person followed and said hastily, "I'm sorry. But did you want the dictionary?"

He was still holding it. "I'm sorry. I didn't mean to walk off with it." He gave the dictionary to her.

"I'll bet I could help you with that word you couldn't find."

He looked down at her. She was very pretty and he found he was smiling at her, despite himself. "You think so?"

"I'm going to try for that prize on the 'Guess What' show tonight," she said earnestly. "Each week they announce a regular subject for the following week. Then they have a special prize for their surprise quest."

Behind him the tall cowboy was still stringing it out with Alma. Bill deliberately delayed. "You're trying for the special prize?"

"Oh, no. The quest has to be announced. Last week the quest was for you to identify a movie star who might pass through your town. Only he never passed through ours. Anyway, the regular subject tonight is ten scrambled definitions of ten hard words. If you think you've guessed the ten words you can telephone in—no matter from how far away. If you get as many as three they'll pay long distance phone charges. If you get all ten right, it's five hundred dollars to the first one phoning! I've been reading the dictionary like mad every night. Go on. Try me."

"What's scopolamine?" Bill asked. "I know it's a medicine—"

"No, it's a drug. Scopolamine is the truth drug. Police use it to make gangsters tell the truth . . ."

It was shattering . . .

When he thought about it he knew that he had known all the time.

The little Hillman Minx throbbed through green hills. It was an afternoon that couldn't be better. Alma rested her blonde head on the hard slope of Bill's shoulder and asked plaintively, "What's wrong? Isn't this fun?"

"Shore," Bill said. "It shore is, Miss."

Alma raised her head. "Honestly! Was I supposed to tell that fella to chase himself?"

"I don't like having you talk to strange guys."

"Well, good Gosh!"

The Hillman purred loudly through a rocky pass. A little later Alma said, "I noticed you weren't wasting your time, either. That girl in jeans was following you around." She returned her head to his shoulder. "She was kinda cute, at that. She was about your age, too. If I was your sister it'd be fun to help you find a cute girl. Why shouldn't you have some fun with a cute girl? You know, you're a lot like my brother was. He was kinda shy making up to cute girls until I helped him get over being so shy."

He moved slightly for her to wriggle more comfortably against him. It was all done without either of them saying anything. The smoothness of her hair pressed against his cheek. His right arm passed over her left arm to the wheel. He could feel her bare arm bend at the elbow, close to his side, to lie softly along his leg; her fingers curled into her palm.

They scarcely exchanged a dozen words between them for the rest of the afternoon. But Bill had a growing conviction that a whole series of doors were silently unlocking and waiting for him to keep on going.

About six-thirty signs began appearing every half mile or so along the highway. Each one announced the Sunset Motel and Hunting Lodge was that much closer. "Stop Here for Good Food & Comfortable Easy-Spring Beds. Only Twenty Miles from Denver."

Bill finally asked, "Why go on to Denver tonight, Alma? Can't we call it a day? We can get up early and be in Denver tomorrow morning when the railway express offices open at nine. What do you say?"

"If you want to," she answered indifferently.

"Are you sore at me?"

"No, I'm not sore at you."

"What's wrong?"

"Nothing," she said crossly. "Sometimes a girl just doesn't want to talk."

The Sunset Motel and Hunting Lodge was more luxurious than Bill had ever anticipated. The view was breathtaking. The sun was vanishing behind the western rim of mountains in a blaze of fire. Their private lodge was five minutes through the pines from the main central lodge and when the assistant housekeeper left them there, Bill saw a maid had been here before them.

The venetian blinds were discreetly drawn. The covers were properly turned back in this bedroom. Bill supposed the covers would be properly turned back on the bed in the other room. Everything was so intimate and so quiet it startled him to hear a squirrel scolding from the pines.

Alma and Bill were still distant with each other and almost too matter of fact. She said she had better fix herself for dinner. He carried her suitcase into the other bedroom as if it was silently understood between them she was to have the bedroom farthest away from the door. Each bedroom had its own adjoining bath and its own radio. After she shut her door he heard music from her radio and water running from her bath.

He stripped and let hot water run into the clean enamel tub in his own bathroom. He shaved. He brushed his teeth. He scrubbed himself, used the comb and hated getting back into the same old clothes. Afterward he waited fifteen or twenty minutes for her. But he was in no hurry. A tide had receded. Later, a moon would arise. He heard her footsteps and she turned off her radio; and next she opened her door. She had brushed her hair until it gleamed like pale gold. Her skin glowed from the bath. His lipstick was a bright pink on unsmiling lips. She gave him a level look.

"Ready?" she asked.

He stepped toward her . . .

She said evenly, "I don't want to be kissed. Let's eat."

The fresh mountain trout was delicious. They had very little to say to each other. When one of them did speak it was politely and almost formally. All through dinner he could not help thinking each minute carried them more closely to the time when they would return to their small discreet private lodge among the pines. He wondered if she also was thinking of it and felt caught by him as he felt caught by her.

They finished dinner by eight. The stars were out. Small electric bulbs twinkled like lesser stars among the pines to guide them along the graveled lane to their own private lodge for the night. Without a word to him she walked into her own bedroom. He heard the radio go on again. He shut and locked the front door. He looked in at her. She had switched on a single reading light over her bed. She was leaning against the wall, listening to the music. She ignored his presence. He remembered how at first that heifer had shied away from the bull. He grew warm.

As casually as possible he said, "Dance?"

She bent over the radio, as if she had not heard him. A thick lock of shimmering hair fell across her forehead. He saw how the linen dress rounded over her small behind and traced the curving line of her thighs until her bare legs came out from the skirt and were a pale amber of calves and delicate ankles to her sandals. She brushed away her hair with her hand and deliberately eyed him a moment and looked back at the radio.

He took her hand and pulled her to him. She came effortlessly into his arms. When the Denver quarter hour of dance music ended and a speech began on the economics of beet production they ceased dancing long enough for him to locate another dance program from a Salt Lake City station. She waited docilely. He could feel her body under the thin linen dress. Although he was certain she was wearing nothing underneath he asked her. She shook her head.

"It's been too hot today." Then she said, "Hold me closer." He couldn't any longer.

She rested her hands on his shoulders, looking up at him. She said, unembarrassed, "Just ignore it. Gosh, we don't have to stop dancing. Don't you think a girl knows anything at all? You should've had a sister."

It gave him a pleasurable thrill when she pressed closer to him. He said, "You talked about things like that with your brother?"

"Why not? Weren't you curious about girls?"

"Well, yes . . ."

"Well, my heavens! Don't you think girls are just as curious about boys? But if a boy doesn't have a sister when he's growing up then he has to find out things from other girls, and sometimes he gets embarrassed or even scared . . ."

"We could pretend you were my sister."

She took an unsteady breath. "Well . . ."

"I just want to look at you."

Her breasts brushed against his arm. "You promise not to make love to me?"

He nodded, speechless.

She stepped back, smiling in an enigmatic way.

The lamp over the bed was a round glow of brightness. She stood in the light like a golden statue. He saw the rapid pulsing on her throat. She lifted an arm and hand to smooth her hair where he had ruffled it removing her dress. The gesture was so graceful and revealing his heart skipped a beat and hammered harder.

"My God, you're beautiful."

"Bill—" She hesitated. "Would you like to dance with me?"

She was smaller, so much smaller than he was. Cautiously, she allowed him to draw her closer. Her skin felt smooth and fresh. When he clasped her she seemed to melt and caress him with such an unimaginable pleasurableness that he stopped trying to be wary.

She jumped away. He stood there, trying to breathe, his legs feeling so weak that he could hardly stand. She was sitting on the bed, her arms raised to lift the tangle of silky hair off her neck, her breath coming very fast.

She trembled violently when he touched her. He would only hold her to himself for an instant.

"Alma, Alma."

"Darling."

Her head fell back on the bed. The lovely shorn hair clustered at her temples like damp petals. His eyes looked down at her; her eyes opened a moment to look up into his before again closing. And it was the most unbelievable surprise to know that they were still two separate people.

Chapter Twelve

They lay side by side in the soft darkness and she listened to his regular and even breathing. All her heart had gone out to him, but could she have been such a fool as to have fallen in love with him? Her thoughts wove a pattern of alternate despair and hope. After all, as he had said, when he became twenty-five she would be only twenty-nine.

Bill had stirred. Perhaps he had awakened. She whispered, "Bill, what happens to us when you get to Sacramento?"

It would serve her right, she thought, if he had been lying and had only sweet talked her into going to bed with him. His voice said firmly, "You're staying with me. We're being married."

"Let's not talk about marriage. It would be heavenly to see each other. You'll have week ends this summer. Can't we do this? I'll want to see some of those old gold-mining towns. I'm gonna—going to enjoy myself. I'll visit one town four or five days; another, the same way, after a couple of weeks. After I settle in a town, let's say I'll get a post card and mail it to you, care of that Sacramento newspaper?"

"Alma, what for? We'll be married."

"I'm so mixed up about us, I need a month or so to decide about marrying you. Right now, let's keep it a secret until I sort myself out. Please? You'll get a post card from me. You'll know the town to meet me. It'll be one of those view cards. I'll sign my initials or maybe just 'A.' You'll just be getting a post card. It might not even be from a girl for all anyone else knows. It's not a letter to get somebody wondering who's writing you, honey. I've been restin' here, thinkin' it all out . . ."

She felt drowsy and languorous. "I'll write something like, 'Having a fine time.' No, I tell you. I'll work in a number, like, 'Saw two swell movies,' or something. That 'two' will mean I'll be waiting for you at two o'clock the day after you get the post card. I'll be waiting at the library like when we met in Omaha. We'll be having our own secret. Bill, it'll be fun. It'll be like being kids again . . ."

It was after ten-thirty when Bill parked the Hillman in front of the main railway express office in Denver. He offered to go in for her. She said, "Thanks, but you can't. Granny shipped it to me. I'll have to identify myself. They won't give it to you. Stay here. I won't be more than five or six minutes."

She kissed him, opened the door before he could argue, and fled into the cavernous building. He settled back in the seat to wait for her. He had risked parking at one of those ten minute unloading and loading openings along the curb. He wasn't certain a passenger car was allowed here. Two big express trucks rushed past the little Hillman, turning two car lengths ahead to the left, to pass on to a cement ramp leading to some interior loading space squeezed in behind the old office buildings and warehouses. He guessed it was all right to wait here a few minutes.

He wished he had a cigarette. He might have time to run across the street to buy a pack. Alma evidently didn't smoke. It was hard to make her out, loving her as he did. To see her she was so quiet and sweet and friendly and yet—instantly it was as if his mind closed iron shutters against any more conjecturing about her. Remembering last night, a whole tide went coursing through him. If this was how it felt to fall in love, it hurt too much.

Alma and he could have a fine good life together. He was convinced he could persuade her to marry him.

A tobacco store was on the opposite corner, directly across from the concrete ramp. It would take him but a minute to run across and buy a pack of cigarettes. The second time he looked toward the tobacco store he happened to see the big grayish man just standing there, near the entrance, half in shadow under a striped awning. It was Sid Gramellini. For possibly two seconds Bill stared. He saw the face with its creased wrinkles like the wrinkles on the skin of an elephant. He didn't know how long Gramellini had been there. He didn't know how Gramellini happened to be here in Denver when Bill had last seen him in the basement office of that glittery clothing store in Omaha. Parked near the tobacco store was a black Buick sedan with a Nebraska license.

Gramellini had one hand in the pocket of his gray tweed coat. The eyes had been watching the entrance of the cavernous building which Alma had entered not more than three minutes ago. Gramellini's eyes swung to Bill and back to the express office.

Bill felt strangled as if by an invisible tourniquet. How blind he had been! He had never wanted to see the truth. Alma! She had to be the reason for all the fantastic events in which he had participated since Saturday; Ed Murvon in the red Dodge, the lemon-blonde girl, the hand-painted tie, the scopolamine, the brassy blonde killed by a hit-and-run driver, the six-hundred-thousand-dollar robbery—everything his mind had resisted against accepting.

Alma! All along he had had an uneasy feeling that she had picked him up too easily. She had changed her mind too quickly about driving to California. He had even asked her if she wasn't running away from something! Who else had she been running away from but Gramellini? It hit Bill all in a flash.

He could imagine Alma walking from the express office, with Gramellini taking that pistol bulging so noticeably in his coat pocket, shooting her, and stepping coolly into the Buick sedan to vanish during the confusion. Perhaps Gramellini's pistol even had a silencer. It was very simple to kill if you killed quickly, a bolt from the blue, and vanished. The girl with brassy hair who might have been Alma had been killed with not much more to it than that, on the library steps that rainy evening in Omaha.

After that, for Bill it was mostly pure reflex. He stepped on the starter. The engine was still warm; it revved at the first crack.

Gramellini was lifting something darkish and not very shiny from the tweed coat. A bee sung loudly. A hole bored through the right-hand side window. In a diagonal line beyond Bill's nose a second hole instantly appeared in the windshield.

Bill wrenched the Hillman into the ramp, then down, squeezed the car by a big truck, and stopped hard. A man in overalls yelled, "Get that heap out of here!"

Bill ignored him. He ran through the side door of the express office. He found himself in a place swarming with great pyramids of boxes, crates, and trunks; some moving on small wheel while pushed by men, others stationary. Voices echoed. A door led into the room beyond.

The next room had counters. There was Alma! She was carrying a leather bag, not seeing him. She was heading toward the entrance—the street entrance.

"Alma!" He had her arm in one hand, the leather bag in the other. "We've got to run for it!" All his life after that in his mind he would connect the smell of stale cabbages with express offices. She came with him unhesitatingly, accepting the emergency as if she had expected it. There was no need for more words. She ran with him.

A truck driver yelled angrily, "Move out. You're blockin' us!"

Bill shoved Alma through the Hillman's door. He looked to his right, up the ramp toward the entrance. Truck horns were shrilling. Near the street a black Buick sedan also had turned in. The Buick was blocked by two trucks before it and another big green truck had swung in behind, off the street. More voices were shouting.

Bill sent the Hillman down the ramp and entered a concrete loading yard. Two men in blue overalls ran furiously to him, shouting. Recklessly, Bill whirled the Hillman to the right toward an opening in the wall. He skinned in front of another growling truck. The opening was an underpass. The hollow whining sound became big for an instant. A train whistled loudly. The whistle changed to a shriek. Bill slammed on the brakes.

He didn't know where he was. A stubby switching engine chugged by him. The engineer leaned out of the window and shouted at him. The engineer's voice was soundless in the confusion. A graveled incline lifted to the right. He took that; there was no place else to go. If he lost time, trying to back to turn around, to get back into the yard, that black Buick would be there. All he could think of was to lose the Buick.

"Bill," Alma had cried out. "What is it?"

That damned gravel incline was petering out. The Hillman was bumping unsteadily over steel tracks.

"Shut up," Bill said violently. "He was waiting to kill you. I saw his gun. We've got to lose him if we can find how to get out of here."

A freight engine was clanking straight at them. Steam spurted. It was like finding himself in one of those nightmares where he went running and running through a maze with strange iron beasts leaping at him. Alma screamed. He tried to turn the steering wheel; but the Hillman's tires wouldn't budge. They were caught in the steel rails. A train whistle pierced his ears. The Hillman jerked violently. Alma was thrown against him. Then the tires mounted the rails; he was driving diagonally, and he turned again, and all at once, the little English car was once more bucketing along a railroad track, while now the freight engine, followed by a line of dusty freight cars went sliding past less than three feet at one side. It was like hearing huge garbage cans being dumped, one after another.

He was driving over a railroad overpass. On one side, below, he could see far underneath a city street with traffic moving in both directions. A man was running toward him, waving his arms. Over to the west he caught a glimpse of a railroad yard, with steel tracks glinting in the sunlight and more switch engines bumping heavily against lines of freight cars.

The yard tender's face blazed crimson in the sunlight. "Geez! You drunk?"

Bill yelled, "How do I get out of here?"

Ahead of him, a semaphore was waving wildly. Round lights glared red like blinking eyes. The man was desperately shoving at a steel gate, rolling on small wheels, like the wheels of a dozen roller-skates. Again, the Hillman's tires resisted. Bill used all his strength. The Hillman rocked and for one dreadful instant Bill could imagine Alma and himself dropping downwards to land into a crashing tangle of steel and splintering glass.

But the Hillman lurched. Bill turned the car sideways. The yard tender was mouthing huge words at them, beckoning. Then the Hillman went lurching through the steel gate. A passenger engine and its red and black line of Pullmans moved past with a sleek, deadly-sounding noise. Bill drove down and into a boulevard and kept going and took four green lights, one block after another, then he cut into north-moving traffic on another highway.

The Hillman seemed to swim with the flow. Presently, Bill turned east, over a rise, through raw new suburbs until he struck a four-lane highway. He covered the next three miles in perhaps four minutes. He lost speed again, at the next long grade.

He risked looking back.

The black sedan was less than half a mile behind.

He said, "I might make the next town before he draws up to us and pours it in. Finding a cop's our only—"

"I can't go to a copper." Her voice was a terrified thin scream.

"It's that bad?" he asked.

"Yes, it's that bad. Go faster!"

"Sixty-two's about our best. That Buick behind us'll probably do ninety."

"Oh, God!"

A gas station slung by, followed by flashings of trees. Next, Bill saw the turn off and took it, the Hillman bounding crazily. There might be a fraction of a chance. A Buick was fast enough, but it was no good for darting into right-angle turns. This was still a macadam road. Didn't this damn mountain country have any narrow dirt roads like you still found in Iowa?

"Alma, can you see the Buick?"

"It followed us off the highway. Now it's on the other side of the hill. I can't—"

"Hang on!"

A side road unexpectedly revealed itself thirty feet ahead. He swung the wheel violently. Sky leaped. A farmhouse a mile away revolved insanely within the frame of the windshield. The rear wheels dug in; gravel sprayed in a solid sheet.

He geared frantically, low to second; back to low; and on through, trying for maximum velocity. The Hillman spurted. Again he shifted through to fourth. They were flying all at once, over the grade. Now they went down on a steep road that was no more than a track overgrown with grass and weeds. For another minute longer the Hillman was still hidden behind the rise from that fleet black sedan. Over a bridge! What luck! Ahead the trail forked three ways like a serpent's tongue forked in old nearly forgotten pictures in an old nearly forgotten book of Bill's childhood.

He ran the Hillman downgrade on the right-hand road and had no idea of where he was going. On each side great trees lifted into the sky like pillars of a cathedral. He twisted the wheel; a line of wire fence rose up before the windshield, twisting crazily. He saw the open gate and heard the scraping of metal as a fender shrieked against wood. But he had guided the little Hillman through the gate, deeper into the trees. He cut the motor, instantly. Silence flooded through the forest like a deep green river.

He scarcely saw Alma, huddled beside him; he listened.

To the west was a droning sound. The black sedan in his mind had become a black dog, running and running after the small rabbit. But here was safety, perhaps. He heard Alma whimper. Now the droning sound of the great eight-cylinder American engine diminished. In another minute it had quite vanished. Gramellini had taken one of the wrong turns! Bill had had two chances to Gramellini's one. Now there would be a respite. How long? In a few more minutes that black sedan would stop; the man inside would decide the Hillman was not on this road. It wouldn't be many minutes before Gramellini drove back to the fork.

Bill backed the Hillman out along the cattle lane to the mountain road and shifted, the little motor singing soft and low. Not too damned fast, he thought. Go quietly! Gramellini mustn't stop somewhere not too far away to listen. Bill coasted half a mile.

He was thankful for being in the foothills of the mountains. At the first crossing he turned right again, by instinct more than anything else, trying to double back.

Now the Hillman picked up speed on a two-lane macadam road that was strung along a narrow valley pointing northeast for several miles. A wall of granite lifted up sheerly, the Hillman's motor moaning out with echoing moans flung from the granite wall.

He glanced at Alma. She had not tried to ask questions during those frightful twenty or so minutes of twisting and darting through the back streets of Denver to find a hole. Not a word had come from her. She knew. Of course she knew. All along, ever since leaving Omaha, the fear must have been growing in her, fear of Gramellini picking up her trail and somewhere finding her. Her own silence convicted her.

Bill said, "We just might have shaken Gramellini. What next?"

"Who?" her voice said.

The two-lane road carried the Hillman through a little mountain town. On one side of the road Bill saw a dozen houses, a few stores, a church with a white cross, a narrow brick building with shuttered windows, and a few more houses flash by, and then the Hillman was climbing. On the other side of the road a canyon was deepening.

"Why keep pretending?" his voice angrily asked her voice. "Sid Gramellini was watching that express office in Denver. He got on our tail—Gramellini—Gramma. You were to meet him, not your grandmother, weren't you?"

"Bill, help me," her voice said. "You told me you loved me."

For a single glance backward his head turned on reflex action. It was still all right. No fleet black sedan was loping behind them. His eyes saw the sun shining bright on the white cross of the little country church with a great greenness of trees and mountains rising up behind it. All within another instant his mind went back in time. He was a boy going to early-morning mass with his father and mother. A voice spoke of love and mercy and forgiveness. While living with an obsessed uncle and a fond weak aunt, Bill had almost forgotten the cool sweet memories of candles burning and a chanting of a great ritual that once had filled his mind with a sense of peace. Even if he was a few years younger than Alma he knew he was the stronger one. He had told her he loved her. He did love her. In those cool dim places of his boyhood all those who had transgressed still found mercy and forgiveness if they came with love and repentance in their hearts. It wasn't too late for Alma and himself. It couldn't be. Desperately he wanted to believe it wasn't.

"I love you. I'm going to do all I know how to help you."

"Gramma'll kill us both if he finds us. Where can we hide?"

"Give me enough pieces to help me think where. When I first read about that armored truck stickup I half convinced myself that a fellow in a red delivery truck, who I'd met early yesterday, was mixed in it. I was wrong, wasn't I?"

"I don't know anyone in a red delivery truck."

"Where does Monk Anzeiger come in?"

"Bill, I didn't know until too late. Honest."

"Don't lie. I'm trying to help you."

"Monk offered me a chance to get a fresh start for myself, out of the country."

"You never went to Drake. You didn't know what a Pulitzer prize was—"

"I did. I was teasing you . . . No, I didn't go to Drake. I worked in a beauty shop off the campus for the last six months. I won't tell you any more about me. But I didn't know there'd be any killing!

Monk claimed he was going to use gas bombs on those fellas. You have to believe me!"

"Where's the money? In that bag you must've shipped to yourself from Council Bluffs? It won't hold six hundred thousand—"

"I've only got a hundred grand. I don't know who got the other five hundred grand. Bill, help me. Run away with me. In a few years you'll be twenty-one. I'll be only twenty-five. Help me and I'll prove I love you, any way you ask. I thought I was so safe. How did Gramma know I'd be in Denver this morning? What will we do?"

His mind was beginning to take hold. He slowed the Hillman to read a road mileage sign and get his bearings again. The road marker informed him: Cynnamon, 6 m. Estes Park (town) 51 m. via Cynnamon. Cynnamon must be a mountain hamlet or town at a main highway junction going north. He remembered the road map he had studied. You could go through Estes Park to strike a main highway west toward Salt Lake City. Or you could keep on north, going westward into Wyoming with a chance of losing yourself somewhere in the northern states long enough to decide what next to do.

"How could Gramma've found me so soon?" she was saying over and over again, like a frightened child.

He shifted to second as the narrow road climbed around another sheer wall of granite. In his mind he saw stacks of newspapers, their pages dating back to that war which had killed his father. Day after day, the news was the same. Vice and rackets had become major industries. Each day the newspapers reported some new disclosures and nobody ever did anything about it. Syndicates mapped out the country for their operations. They dealt in women, drugs, theft, death, horror, and filth exactly as other great corporations dealt in automobiles or shoes or breakfast foods. It had become so commonplace there was no longer anything fantastic in their communication nets and interlocking directorates until you stopped and thought of it.

A phrase came to Bill's mind, "the moral disintegration of America," which his sociology teacher had often repeated to a bored class of kids who didn't really give a damn. The trouble was nobody any more gave a damn except people like Gramellini, who hid what he was doing behind a glittering store front. Gramellini had not even been very original in using a clothing store as a front. In the newspapers you could read any day almost of other lords of vice and rackets hiding behind similar stores or haberdasheries. They had long-since moved out of back rooms in bars or offices in fancy houses. There was a horrible cunning in selecting a front that was ubiquitous, even a little absurd, such as a clothing store. As far as Bill knew there could be a hundred or a thousand other innocuous glittering stores of one sort or another in that many other cities. It was no more fantastic than to read, only a few days ago, he remembered, of the latest newspaper disclosure on organized murder. Buying control of an insurance company! After Bill had walked right into Gramellini's arms in Omaha, perhaps all Gramellini had done was to put in a few long-distance phone calls to trace Alma's flight. Bill felt his mind go rigid. No. His reasoning was missing something. *Gramellini was here, himself. He hadn't sent a hired killer.* Why? Gramellini was on this job, himself.

He heard Alma say, "If Gramma found me once, he will again. I want to live. *Think* of something!" she begged. "Please! *Please!*"

"I've got to know everything you know if we expect to find a way out. What about Council Bluffs?"

"I was terrified that day. I don't like telling you."

"You wanted me to get rid of the blue Plymouth for you? You expressed the money bag to yourself in Denver to be safe if you were stopped when crossing the bridge to Omaha. I've guessed that much. You shook me off at the Council Bluffs Hotel. You had money to buy a car from a second-hand dealer. But why," he asked, "didn't you ditch me?"

"I fell for you."

"Don't lie."

"Bill, you have to believe me. *I'm here with you.* I did come to you in Omaha instead of ditching you, didn't I?"

That was true. She was here with him and she could have run away from him. He turned north on a three-lane highway that passed through the town of Cynnamon. High in the sky a mountain peak was dazzling white from the snow still unmelted on it. The air smelled fresher. He was beginning to hope Alma and he just might have a fair chance of getting to Wyoming and losing themselves there. It was worth the try. Evidently Gramellini had no hoods along with him. Gramellini was alone on this job. But why? There was something abnormal and beyond reasoning to think of a lord of vice and rackets going out on a limb himself to catch up with a girl. There was no sense to it—unless somehow Alma had exploded a big frame Gramellini had planned, so that Gramellini was now forced to handle the pickup job himself. Had there been something exquisitely and carefully planned by Gramellini in connection with that big holdup? Had Alma smashed it for him?

Bill said, "Listen, Alma. We can't just keep running forever. Give me a little help. Fill in for me. What about Monk Anzeiger? Were you and he supposed to deliver the hot money to that grocery store?"

"Yes. But Monk had only a hundred grand, I tell you. Before we reached Atlantic, Monk got the news broadcast that he'd been identified. It was the first I knew that—that those fellas had been killed. Oh, please believe me! Then Monk got out. He said I had to drive to Atlantic to deliver to Gramma. I was scared. I saw you—"

"But Gramma wasn't there, though."

"That charged me up like a kite. I didn't know what to do."

"You know Gramellini?"

"Bill, I just met him once for a coupla minutes in Des Moines. He frightened me. All I knew about him he was Monk's boss.

"He wasn't in that store. It doesn't make sense, does it? That was when I started thinking there was a frame. You told me that girl had blonde-colored hair. Remember? I got to thinking maybe somebody had switched signals and I was to be blasted down soon's I entered that store. So I just began running."

He gave a start. He had to watch the road as it swung lazily over a stone bridge and through another winding pass. The lemon blonde in that crummy store! He had walked into that dingy little Iowa store with that lemon blonde and the hood waiting in there had been going to shoot them both. That afternoon, in Omaha, the brassy-haired girl waiting on the library steps had been brutally killed, run over. Both times, a mistake had been made. Both times a death trap had been set for Alma. That was the connection between the three blonde-haired girls which had throbbed in his mind ever since Saturday night. What else? There was something else.

He shifted gears again. The Hillman was great going downhill but nothing much in these mountains for speed. He felt a rush of pity for Alma. She had said miserably, "So I just began running." What chance had she ever had? Men like Gramellini parceled out the country to themselves and no one cared or did anything about it. You could think of Gramellini as being one of the horrors, one of the great black dogs to chase the sheep of the nation. Gramellini had his own private army. He was a general in this continuing and vicious war. He borrowed all the stale signals and hackneyed subterfuges used in open wars, too, for his own thugs to recognize each other. What else? Bill was quite sure that he knew all the connections now.

"Alma—that tie you gave me. Where did you get it?"

"Why?"

"Just don't lie. Please. It's too important."

"It was Monk's."

"Monk's?"

"Yes."

Alma told him how Monk had changed clothes in the willow grove last Saturday morning. He didn't look at her face. He felt a stabbed sensation.

He said, "Gramellini bought that tie for Monk to wear?"

"He bought all Monk's clothes. Monk told me that Gramellini bought the clothes for all the boys in the mob."

"Don't you know who Gramellini is?"

"God, I told you. Bill. I only saw him that once in Des Moines—"

"I met him."

He felt her move convulsively. "You met him?" It was a cry.

"You sent me to him."

"You're crazy. I *never* did. Geez, Bill! It's bad enough without having you—"

"Listen," he said quietly, hearing his voice slide over the running murmur of the Hillman. "You sent me to him. Maybe you didn't know it, but you did. He uses a clothing store in Omaha as a front. He owns Crabtree's."

"Crabtree's?"

"Didn't you know?"

"I never, I never . . ." She sounded hysterical. He reached blindly for her hand.

"Please, Alma—"

"Bill, I never knew. Believe me."

"I do."

"I never knew Gramma owned Crabtree's. I wouldn't have sent you there if I did."

"I know you wouldn't have. Now, listen. Let's get back to that trick tie of Monk's. There's a connection. Wouldn't that tie've marked Monk to any hoodlum sent to shoot him down?"

"It was a frame, wasn't it?"

"A hell of a big one if we're guessing right."

"Monk never would've suspected that rotten tie was supposed to spot him to some hood . . ." Her voice broke. "And I gave it to you! You *have* to believe me. I didn't know. I didn't!" She pulled her hand from his and covered her face with both hands. "Oh, Bill, help me. I'll be good. I'll be decent. I just want a chance to live like other girls. Please!"

If Alma and he were in a nightmare, he thought, it was no more than a fragment of the great nightmare which must have trapped hundreds of frightened and bewildered people. How filthy the world had become when it was no longer at all fantastic to read every day in the newspapers that conditions were like this, and have no one try to do anything at all to put a stop to them.

"Don't you see?" he told her. "Gramellini must have snatched *six hundred thousand* dollars out of that truck. Yes. Hell, yes, it's a frame. I can't see all the details yet. Perhaps he had a chance to use drugs—scopolamine—to get somebody to talk. *I* don't know. That's not so important right now. Maybe he bribed the driver and guards to deliver five hundred thousand dollars of the shipment at a first stop . . . Could Monk's small mob be supposed to fake a second holdup? Why not? Remember? That newspaper said the state cop was shot from *the rear*. The armored truck crowd *killed* the cop. They *were* expecting a holdup. Gramellini *had* mentioned gas bombs. The armored truck guys were in the thing. But it was a double-cross. Monk's small mob killed them. Then Monk took the hundred thousand, never knowing the five hundred thousand had been passed on to Gramellini previously."

"Bill, it might be. I just don't know."

"It has to be. It ties in, doesn't it? You and Monk were supposed to go to that store and get killed. It would have been a perfect triple-cross. Police would've found a hundred thousand at the store and rooted around for the other five hundred thousand. But the trail would've stopped right there, with you and Monk dead! That was where the comic-strip tie came into the scheme—it identified Monk to the two hoods, a couple of paid killers. Those killers wouldn't even have known about the money—not a thing except they were to knock off a guy and his girl, and run."

"But there were two other fellas in Monk's mob."

"What do you think? They scattered, didn't they? Couldn't each one have walked into a killer waiting in a strange place? It's a complete frame, Alma. Gramellini ends with half a million, no one even knowing he has it, the guards killed, Monk's mob supposedly wiped out. The police would still have been swarming around that store—and the whole scheme's all gone to hell because Monk *didn't* go to the store. He jumped out. He sent you. You gave me a lift. The storekeeper slammed the hood with a meat cleaver. It was all a whirley-gig mix-up, and you grabbed the hundred thousand supposed to be left for the police to find as a red herring. Now Gramellini knows you've made off with that hundred thousand. If you're stopped and caught by the police—Don't you see? The police'll have a direct line through you to Monk and Gramellini and the whole triple-cross. Gramellini's own syndicate'll learn that their own top man tried to nab half a million for himself, without splitting. Gramellini *has* to get you. He can't let any hood try. He's stuck, himself."

"Bill—stop talking. I'm gonna get sick."

"You've got to hang on and listen if we're ever going to find an out in this filthy mess. How many years has Gramma been planning a half million foolproof grab? I don't know. He's got that store as a front with those queers fronting him in the store.

It'd make anyone sick to think of it. He's in a vice racket. Now, all at once perhaps, he's about finished. I heard he was nearly indicted. His name's been mentioned in the papers. People know about him. Why isn't he in the same jam that other bigtime hoodlum on the coast was—the one who got too much publicity? Maybe Gramellini's due for a shift from his bosses. Maybe he's going to be dropped off his deal and somebody else put in above him? So—he's tried for that half million on his own. Does that make sense? But you've blown it for him unless he can get hold of you and stop you—"

The little Hillman's engine coughed, stuttered, and for a paralyzing instant Bill thought the English car was going to stop. Then the engine picked up. But Alma cried, "Oh, God! The gas tank's empty. We forgot to get gas!"

Chapter Thirteen

He shifted to neutral to let the Hillman coast down the long grade and shifted back, the motor revved again, at the next ascent. Once more the motor stuttered. He pulled at the choke. Alma cried, "Isn't that a gas station up there? Can we make it?"

They almost didn't.

It wasn't much of a station, either. The new sign on the roof said, *"Aksarben Last Chance Stop."* There was a single gasoline pump, a second and larger for diesel oil for trucks, with a lunchroom behind the pumps, and the man was as slow as molasses. While he pumped in gas, Bill stuck out his head and sighted down the long grade behind them.

Twenty or thirty miles away along the southeast horizon, between two purple rises of mountains, he saw the city of Denver. It was like a small labyrinth in which the houses and buildings had become indistinct. Only the crisscross pattern of streets was still visible. Far below the gas station, a few cars and a truck or so had topped a lower rise. They were now plugging up the longer grade. Among none of those seemingly tiny vehicles for children to play with was a fleet black sedan.

He felt Alma grasp his arm and turned. Her eyes were huge with the unspoken and terrifying question in them. He shook his head. It looked as if they had shaken Gramellini. For how long? Bill couldn't help thinking. In his mind he could again see him drawing that silent pistol when he had been standing there under the awning of the cigar store. There had been something glacial in his self-confidence. He had only Alma and an eighteen year old kid riding with her to deal with. There had been nothing for him to fear. Bill wished he had a gun—anything. God, how helpless he felt!

The lanky gasoline station man finally finished. It was eight gallons. These little furrin' cars never held much gas, did they? Bill said brusquely how much? It was two dollars and thurty-two cents. Gas cost more in the mountains. Why didn't he hurry? The man was taking all day to make change. Bill asked how to get on the main road through to Cheyenne and Wyoming and immediately wished he hadn't because the man had to stop counting change and scratch his head. He heard Alma whisper agonizedly, "Have him hurry!"

But the man was pointing. He said, "You folks should've taken Highway Eighty-seven out of Denver. You folks were too far west. The best thing you folks could do would be to go north to Beetrock and turn east on the Estes Park road to Loveland and then pick up the north highway. But you folks had best watch out for the detour sign five miles from here. The bridge was being repaired at Spire Rock pass and the dumb road fellers had gone on strike so you had to go west through Bensonville on the detour."

"Thank you," Bill said. He stepped on the starter.

"Wait—here's your change. Now, lemme see. You give me five dollars, didn't you?" His slowness was infuriating.

The man counted the money. "Watch fur that detour. If you go into Spire Rock pass you'll have trouble turnin' around. You two must be strangers to Colorady, gettin' so far off the main road. I'm nearly a stranger here m'self. Only moved here last month. From Nebrasky. Got my sign there, Aksarben'—Nebrasky backwards. M' wife likes it here but I miss old Omaha. I still listen to them Omaha radio shows, even. Only last night—"

"We're in a hurry," Bill said, reaching out his hand. "Do you mind?"

"Oh, sure. You give me five dollars an'—" The man stared at Bill and across at Alma as if thunderstruck, "Say! I bet you're the blonde couple they talked about, in that surprise quest on the 'Guess What' radio show last night?"

Bill said stupidly, "What?" as if held by shock or inertia from the shock.

"Why, the feller announced a young couple would be drivin' through Nebrasky towns in a Hillman Minx. Catch was, there'd be *three* separate couples drivin' three diffrunt Hillmans. To win the hundred-dollar special prize you had to identify the

Hillman with the right license plate. See? Each Hillman had a license plate from a diffrunt state. The radio feller didn't say which Hillman got you the prize. You had to ask when you stopped the car. You got a Ioway license. You an' your wife—or is she your sister?—are both real light-haired. By Jings! you *must* be one of them radio couples! Tell me. Did that 'Guess What' feller send you two into Colorady to wait a couple days before drivin' back to Nebrasky to be identified—"

"Bill!" came Alma's strangled voice from where she had twisted to look out of her window toward the long grade behind them. *"Look!* Isn't that the black sedan?"

The man was speaking, but his words seemed to trail off into an insane jumble as Bill looked back. Half a mile away, possibly, at the bottom of the long grade he saw a miniature truck and behind it, still very much like those tiny plastic automobiles sold for children, were five cars bunched in a line behind the truck. The last one was a black sedan. It could be a Buick. Now all at once the black sedan turned out and streaked along the other line, turning in sharply ahead of the truck, just in time to escape crashing head on into a car flying down toward Denver.

Bill stepped hard on the gas. The last thing he saw of the station attendant was a startled face, the jaw gaping, silver dollars and quarters spraying up into the sunlight. The Hillman would do no better than fifty-two on the long grade. Bill heard himself shouting, "How far behind?"

"It's stuck behind another truck. But Gramma must've seen us. Bill, stop. We'll get out and run—"

"He'd pick us off with that pistol. Duck down on the floor. I'm going to try for Spire Rock pass!"

"Are you crazy? That man told us the bridge was down!"

"Do what I say. It's one chance we've got!"

Even as he had been shouting to her an idea had begun desperately shaping itself in his head. Perhaps it was madness. He was past caring. He had an unbelieving sensation. It was like being probed by invisible fingers. The Hillman rattled and bucketed as he let the little engine rev full out in second gear to go over the top of the grade.

How Gramellini had arranged to have them described on the "Guess What" radio show last night, Bill didn't know. It didn't matter how. Probably it would have been arranged through a series of friends or satellites connected in the fringes of the syndicate's big operations. It would have had to be managed deviously, on the X to Y to Z principle. The program director in charge of the Omaha program no doubt would never suspect that his last night's surprise quest had been altered hastily, with another substituted, possibly even by the sponsor as an amusing favor for some influential politician, as a coldly calculated method of quickly tracing two young people trying to escape in a Hillman Minx.

The top of the grade was approaching; now it was less than fifty yards away. He threw the gear into low, the Hillman's little mill whining louder. He recalled that young person in jeans, back there in that country store. She had been a "Guess What" radio fan. Perhaps she had been the one to phone in last night to say a Hillman Minx with an Iowa license had stopped at her father's store. Now the Hillman had gone over the grade and Bill lost perhaps two precious seconds by slowing down, steadying the wheel, and casting a look behind him. The great descent of road fell away to the south behind him, a ribbon of blackish blue under the sun; and far down, the black sedan had turned in at the "Aksarben" gas station. Even in that instant, the black sedan began pulling away from the station. Gramellini would have learned that the Hillman had stopped for gas less than five minutes ago.

Through the windshield Bill saw a big painted road sign: "Emergency Detour. Bensonville 22 m." An arrow pointed to a road going west. That was the detour the gas station attendant had warned Bill not to miss. He slowed down instead of shooting ahead to the west. Alma cried, "Don't stop! Maybe there's a town we can get to . . ." But there wasn't any town they could get to, not for twenty-two more miles. To block the Spire Rock highway a plank had been placed across two whitely painted trestles. An unlit lantern hung from the plank. Beyond the block the highway swung to the northeast, vanishing between the sides of two sheer rises of mountain covered by a tangle of trees and thickets.

She screamed, "What are you doing? You can't go that way!"

He steered the Hillman around the left-hand trestle, going over a crumbling shoulder of loose dirt.

"Oh, God, the service station man told us we'd be stuck. The bridge is out!"

He had to drive with one hand, grabbing at her with the other. She was trying to open the door on her side to jump. "We can't keep running."

"He'll kill us. He'll shoot us down like flies. Monk told me. Gramma practices that way. He'll shoot at flies on a wall—"

"Do what I say. Listen to me!"

The idea had leaped larger in his mind. All of a sudden he felt emptied of everything but that one possibility that had come to him. They couldn't keep running. He knew that, now. You had to make a stand somewhere.

The great walls of Spire Rock canyon rushed fluidly on either side of the Hillman; and now, ahead, he saw the rusted arches of an old bridge come into view. He put his foot down to the floorboard and the Hillman leaped and noise echoed and next he gave the brake all it would take, feeling himself lift from the seat, with Alma thrown against him. She was still screaming. The Hillman skidded, fish-tailing back and forth across the macadam. For that long dreadful second he was afraid he had misjudged his speed.

Another road block was there. The planks swarmed up at the Hillman. He spun the steering wheel. He braked the Hillman near a big pine on the side of the road, jumped out—the road lunging off behind him through Spire Rock pass was still empty. He had no idea how many seconds or minutes more of grace he had. Alma had leaped from her side. He thought she was going to crumple right there. He caught her by the arms.

"Climb up to those trees," he ordered. "Off there, to the right."

"I can't—"

"You've got to."

"He'll shoot us down like flies on a wall—"

"He's a city man, Alma. Just listen to me. I'm country. I'm used to rocks and trees. All I want is five seconds after he arrives. Hide!"

"God, I can't. I'm gonna be sick—"

He kissed her, holding her strongly for another instant. "Wait till he gets here and gets out. Then yell. Hear? Yell, Alma. If you love me—if we've any chance—yell like hell. Make him look for you. Now, run!"

A sudden drone began echoing from far away through the pass. She gave a start. He shoved her toward the other side of the road. He watched her run and start climbing up the side of the cliff and the droning sound came bigger and bigger. He whirled and started upwards on the side which reared above the tree and Hillman. He had noticed a ledge up there, twenty or thirty feet above the road. If only he could reach it and be hidden before the black sedan came surging down toward the broken bridge!

He heard Alma's shrill cry. He twisted around, grasping a tree root. Fragments of shale spilled over his head and arms. He heard her cry despairingly to him. Over there on the other side she was like a small doll, all white with tousled yellow hair, against the grey-black rocks under the pines. Some giant might have carelessly tossed her up there. She had thought Bill was following after her.

With all his force he shouted, "For God's sake, do what I told you. Hide in the trees. It's our one chance!"

Perhaps at last she understood what he meant to attempt for all at once she was crawling up and up. She vanished. The sound of the unseen Buick's engine reverberated through the pass like distant thunder. Now it was too late for him to go higher. He hunched down behind a tilted pine whose roots had dug deeply into the loose shale. The sun was like fire. Frantically he tried to claw a shallow space for himself. Shale loosened behind and above him, tumbling over him. He lay there, unmoving. The Buick had curved out from Spire Rock pass.

Brakes squealed.

Tires whined.

That meant that Gramellini had seen the Hillman Minx and the arch of broken bridge half spanning the gorge. A jay cried and was silent.

Next, Bill heard the crunching of footsteps on the shale below him. What the hell was wrong? You could imagine you were hearing someone walking with four or five feet, like some unnatural beast, not a two-legged man. Bill risked lifting his head—and was seized by a convulsion of agony.

There were two men down there, not one!

Gramellini was standing near the Buick with the heavy patience of the hunter, his right hand holding a blue-black pistol with something like a bulbous snout attached to the end of the barrel.

But the second man was moving warily away from the Buick toward the other side of the canyon. Now the second man had paused, to glance upward.

Bill dropped flat, his arms and legs twitching. It was frightful. He damned himself. He should have seen the driver in that Buick. He had never once thought of there being two men. How had he so badly missed? What chance was there now? He heard Gramellini's thick assured voice, "Start climbing, Monk. Stick your rod in your pocket and watch yourself while getting up those rocks. And goddamn it, don't fall! I'm covering you. Look! That piece of cloth. Isn't that from the girl's dress?"

Bill felt his body jerk. Gramellini had named the man, "Monk." Monk Anzeiger! The killer was here, too, along with the big man who pulled all the strings. Bill had assumed Gramellini would be by himself. But somehow, somewhere, Gramellini had managed to pull in Monk Anzeiger. How certain Gramellini had appeared down there during Bill's brief shocked glimpse of the two men. Why shouldn't he be? To have a killer do away with a helpless unarmed foolish girl and the boy she had picked up would be no more than a trivial business item for someone such as a Mr. Sidney Gramellini. To kill quietly and to terrorize efficiently were merely standard business tactics in his successful line of commercial ventures. No one ever had done anything about it in the past. Why should anyone care now, or object, if a silly girl and a romantic boy were quietly and neatly done away with?

Bill listened. Sweat prickled into his eyes. Oh, my God, there was no chance at all. He felt lax. He wanted to stay there, to hide, never to move. He had no will or courage at all. Everything was lost. And he had ordered Alma to attract attention to herself, hoping in that split second when she called out that Gramellini would be distracted enough for Bill to leap. But he had never counted on the two of them. He listened. A jay cried more piercingly.

"Monk!" From the far side of the pass sounded Alma's thin wail of terror. "Monk, don't shoot me. Mr. Gramellini—don't—let—"

Bill never heard the rest. He had to go on with what he had planned. There was nothing else left for him to do.

He jumped.

He landed upon massive shoulders with such force that Gramellini foundered instantly. Bill was on him, striking, slamming down to the ground with him, grabbing at that pistol. He jumped up, backing away. The world reeled. He saw Monk up there, going up the side of the cliff, arms spread-eagled.

"Hold it," Bill shouted.

For another instant there was a sensation of everything going rigid. He saw Monk's head slowly and precariously turn, the eyes sighting down and back toward him through the heavy horn-rimmed glasses. From somewhere higher, Alma was crying, "Bill, he'll shoot!"

But right then, Monk could not shoot. He was using both hands and feet to climb toward Alma. Now he was caught. If he loosened a hand to reach for his gun, Bill could shoot first. Bill sighted back down at his feet at the unmoving body and felt himself waver. Gramellini lay there, the big gray head having the look of a partly broken eggshell. Gramellini would never rise of his own efforts again. It must have been instantaneous. The grayish head had fallen on one of the sharp pointed lava segments; it had been like falling on a spike.

Bill walked forward stiff-legged, and said, "So you're Monk Anzeiger?"

"I'll make a deal with you, boy," said the hoarse voice.

Bill pointed the pistol. "Don't move, Monk. Freeze. If you move, I'll plug you . . ." Cautiously he reached up his left hand, grabbed at the .45 automatic where Monk had shoved it in the coat pocket, and flung the automatic as far as he could over his shoulder. He stepped back. He saw Alma's white face looking down upon them.

"All right, Alma," he said.

But Alma cried, "Bill, watch out—"

Monk let go, dropped the five or six feet to the road, whirled, faced Bill and said, "Gimme a break, kid," and started running toward the bridge. He stopped where the bridge had fallen away, wavered, caught himself, and sighted toward a shelf of rocky shale extending a yard or so parallel to the bridge. Bill had leveled his pistol; but he simply stood there, white of face, his eyes like blue fire, discovering he was incapable of shooting down an unarmed man from the back.

Monk gathered himself all within that moment of time, leaped prodigiously, and landed on the shelf of rock and immediately began scrambling upwards like a big monkey. Bill heard Alma crying out to him. He felt transfixed. He was too damn chicken. He wasn't any good as a killer. He had even had unwilling admiration for the man's courage to attempt that leap. Monk grasped at tree roots, hauled himself to the top, and looked back, down at Bill. And Bill looked up at him. Monk gave him a mocking salute, raising a hand—and vanished into the great trees.

Alma said viciously, "You let him go?"

Bill turned slowly. Yes, he supposed he had. What the hell did it matter? How far would Monk get by himself, on foot, unarmed, in these mountains, with every newspaper in the country probably printing pictures of him, all the police and sheriffs alerted? He looked around and saw Gramellini, dead, and shivered. Alma was staring at him.

Slowly he walked past the dead man and picked up Monk's automatic. There just might be a chance that Monk would not run for it but perhaps even now was peering at them from somewhere up there. Bill had a notion Monk would keep on running, hoping to find a hiding place, somehow, somewhere. But you never could tell. Oh, Jesus! He felt it taking him. Too late he wished he had not been chicken. Damn them for hauling Alma into such a rotten mess. He should have killed Monk with no compunction at all.

He asked her unsteadily, "Can you shoot?"

She was trembling. "Not much. A little."

"Do this. Stand there, away from that cliff. If Monk's up there don't give him a chance to jump as I did and surprise us."

"What—" She seemed to reel. She was making a tremendous effort. He saw the beat of blood on her temples. "Bill, what are you going to do?"

He gave her Monk's automatic. "I think he's probably putting as much distance behind him as possible. If he isn't and is up there, watching down, he'll see the two of us are armed. He won't have the chance I had of catching anyone by surprise. I'm thinking about you. That's all I'm thinking about. I can't help if it's wrong. Stay put. Watch for Monk."

Then he began dragging Gramellini's body to the car. He pushed. He shoved. The body sagged. Bill's lungs were on fire. He started the Buick, feeling the massive weight of the body go against him. The Buick had one of those automatic shifts. That helped. He got the Buick rolling, with the dead man there in the front seat. Then—Bill jumped away and heard a splintering sound of boards breaking. The Buick had lunged through the barrier. The front wheels dropped through the open space; the black length of metal went sliding downwards. It vanished. Finally, there came a small crashing noise from deep down in the gorge. Then there was only a silence. Bill scanned the west ridge of the cliff. He saw no sign at all up there of Monk Anzeiger. He went to Alma. She stared back at him, seeming to waver.

He said, "We can't go to the police as long as we've got that money. We've got to send that money back as proof we had no intention of stealing the stuff."

"No, Bill. No! It might be days before someone even reports a car was driven off the bridge into the gorge. Don't you see? We are safe! Monk's got to go into hiding. He won't ever bother us. What can he do, unarmed, on foot, no car, in all these miles of mountain roads? Bill, maybe you were smart not to shoot Monk. The less we're involved the better. All he can do is try to hide. He won't bother about us any more. Bill! We are safe. We are!"

"We aren't and never will be until we've sent the money in that bag back to Boone, Iowa. When that's done, I've got to let the police know Monk Anzeiger's somewhere in this part of—"

"Bill—" She stepped away from him. "I won't ever give up all that money! It's mine, now."

Even while she helped wipe blood from his scratches and he brushed shale dust and grime from his clothes to make himself halfway presentable they began to argue.

They drove a good sixty miles through winding roads, Bill having an uneasy feeling grow in his mind. Even if it was foolish of him to think that Monk Anzeiger might try to follow he was determined to get far enough away, by enough devious roads, to lose themselves. Crossing high above a mountain stream, Bill threw the silenced pistol and the .45 automatic from the car window.

It was middle afternoon when he drove into the remote little mountain town of Besonville. Alma said wearily, "Do you have to keep going and going on these rotten roads? I'm bushed."

"I just want to get far enough from Rock Spire pass—"

"Bill, I just don't understand you. Monk's going to have to think of saving his own skin, isn't he? We're finished with him."

"I think so, too, but I had to make sure. We can wash up some place here if you like and head north, this evening, for Estes Park and the road west toward Nevada."

"We've wasted hours."

"No, I wanted to be certain Monk Anzeiger wouldn't follow us. Let the police nab him a thousand miles from wherever you and I are."

"Bill, I'm tired arguing about that money and the police. Can't we find a place not too close to town where we can have baths and get our breaths and—and try to talk over things sensibly? I know I'm acting nasty, the way I've been nearly screeching at you."

Chapter Fourteen

The Rockcrest Cottage Camp at the western end of town looked secluded. Evidently there wasn't much business because a sign, "Camp for Sale Cheap—Good Bargain", hit your eyes as soon as you drove through the opening of a hedge that had been allowed to go wild. The owner was a snaggle-toothed man of at least sixty and he had been sitting there in a cluttered office playing cards with a fat woman whose hair was dyed a purplish shade of red. Bill almost left, but Alma looked so wan and fragile his heart went out to her with renewed anxiety. The reaction from what had happened in

Spire Rock pass was hitting her. It was hitting him, too. He wouldn't have liked to admit how drained he felt. And on top of everything else there had been that bitter acrimonious violent argument between them about what to do with the money. Their nerves were at the breaking point. It would be a mistake to go on until they had time to rest and attempt to put themselves back together again, to talk it over quietly.

The snaggle-toothed man spun a dog-eared register around for Bill. He cast an appreciative glance at Alma and said, "Jist sign here. What name you sign don't matter. Mirandy and me ain't nosey. Maybe this motel ain't so much t' look at. But those fancy motels and camps at the east of town are mostly filled with lungers and like to pry. We've had young couples from Denver stoppin' here before. They don't bother us and we don't bother 'em. How long you want a cottage? It's the same price for the night or a couple hours."

Bill stiffened. He said, "For tonight, if you don't mind," and deliberately wrote, "Mr. and Mrs. William Owens, Jr., Sacramento, Cal." in the register. It was almost true. It would be true in a few more days. It gave him a thrill off pride to write it that way, too. Even the old man's attitude subtly changed. The suggestion of lewdness vanished from the cracked old voice.

"Yes, sir, Mr. Owens. It's too early yet in the afternoon for most tourists to begin hunting a place for the night. You got the camp to yourself. I'll show your wife and you our best cottage. It's ten dollars. Sure, pay now. That's our rule."

Alma and Bill returned to the car and drove slowly along a weedy graveled path, around what once might have been a rock garden, and past a line of ragged acacia trees, while the snaggle-toothed old man walked ahead to lead the way. Their cottage was secluded enough from the road. But if it was the best one in the motel camp, Bill was thankful Alma and he had arrived early and did not have to take any of those that were presumably second choice. He got out, carrying the heavy leather bag in one hand and Alma's suitcase in the other. She slung her coat across one shoulder, her shorn hair like flax in the bright mountain sunlight. Sometimes he would almost forget how slight and delicate she looked until he would happen to notice her with the sun shining on her, or against a background of deep green trees, and all over again have a warm proud delight of knowing he loved her and she loved him. There was going to be a chance for them. It wasn't too late. They could have a good life together if only she would understand the money must be quickly returned.

The old man was being apologetic about the cabin. In one corner was a pile of magazines and old newspapers which, he said, would only take him a minute to clear. The couple who'd been here last month on a vacation hadn't done nothing but lie abed and read and play a radio to all hours of the night 'stead of enjoying themselves by fishing, like most touristers did. His wife had a heart condition. He guessed she hadn't quite tidied up the place. He could have everything fixed in a jiffy.

Alma slung her coat on the back of a chair and gave Bill a half amused, half rueful smile. Bill dropped the heavy bag on the table and Alma's on the other chair and said, "No, thanks. Don't bother," and walked with the old man to the door to get rid of him. But he thought of something. He asked, "Is there an express office in town?"

"If you want to send a parcel you'll have to go to the Red Line bus stop jist east of the liberry. They'll ship any parcel for you on through to Denver and the reg'lar express."

Bill closed the door, listening to the shuffling footsteps fade away on the gravel. He locked the door and looked across at Alma in the dimness of the room and then at the leather bag on the table.

"The money's in there?" he asked.

"Open it," she said.

He went to the table. "It's locked."

"No. Just push that brass knob."

He opened the bag. It was crammed full of flat packets of crisp green notes. He had never seen so much money in all his life. He felt Alma's shoulder touch his arm as she waited silently at his side. His heart was racing. There was even a crumpled Federal Reserve piece of flimsy paper on which a total of the various denominations had been typed, with a signature scrawled by an unknown person. One hundred thousand dollars! It was plenty for two people to live on in luxury all their lives. He felt the shakes taking him.

Alma's voice said, "Darling, isn't it a tremendous lot of money? What a wonderful time we could have. We're safe now. It's ours."

Bill shut the bag, hearing the brass catch click dryly. A fly buzzed loudly in the still hot air. He seemed to see that black Buick plunging down into a chasm. Again Monk was grinning down at him before vanishing into a greenness. Bill desperately wanted a surcease from terror and from running. More than ever, he knew he was right. Alma's and his chance to make something of each other and have a good life depended upon getting rid of that money and of starting fresh.

With a strained calmness she was asking, "Why did you want to know where the express office is?"

"We've got to ship the money back."

"Darling, I'm not going to fight with you about it, now. You're so tense and drawn it makes me want to cry to look at you. Let's have our baths. I want fifteen or twenty minutes to shut my eyes and not move. I want fresh clothes on me. After that, I might be ready to try to eat something. Can't we talk it out quietly, then? Please, darling?"

"Well. All right."

Perhaps he had jumped her too fast. He would give her time. They both needed time to take off some of the compression. He felt like hell. He didn't like to think how she must feel.

The bathroom had a concrete floor and had been built of heavy pine planks, evidently added to the cottage as an afterthought. The daylight seeped in so dimly from a small narrow ventilating slit under the ceiling that Bill looked around for the electric-light switch. There was none. As his eyes adjusted to the semidarkness he saw an old-fashioned brass candle holder on the top of the toilet's flushing tank, with a stump of candle and a few matches stuck in the slot. A shower head dripped water into an old galvanized tub. The place smelled of dampness and fungus. The water ran coolish from both hot and cold faucets.

When he returned to the bedroom, Alma had partially undressed. He had an indescribable sensation of well-being to have her so unconcerned by him seeing her. It was as if they actually were married. She had opened her suitcase, laying out his comb and brush on the old bureau. She said, "I'll hurry, darling."

"You don't have to hurry."

"I'd forgotten. We don't have to run any more, do we?"

She kissed him. He began removing his woolen shirt. It felt sticky. He had no other. He had meant to buy clothes this morning in Denver. He heard her splashing in the tub. "Bill," she called. "Please soap my back. Do you mind? I will yours, when it's your turn. The water feels so good."

The soap lathered abundantly in this mountain water. Her white skin had a moist fresh smell and she clasped her hands behind her head to hold her hair away from the water and her color was beginning to return to her cheeks.

"I love you so damn much," he said.

"Oh, Bill. I know we can be happy together. We've got everything we want. All you have to do is be reasonable."

It was as if she had plunged a needle into his heart.

"It's no go, Alma, not with that money hanging over our heads. No, thanks. It just won't work out."

"It will. If you send the money back and spill to the coppers about Monk you know what that means, don't you? It'll mean the coppers'll know about me. I'd die before being hustled off to jail for years." Her eyes were very blue and frightened. "Is that what you want?"

He shook his head. He felt himself foundering. He couldn't endure the thought of Alma being sent to jail. Even now he wanted to take her into his arms. Her skin glistened. It was like warm ivory. She was all pink and white from her bath and her hair curled damply.

"Listen, Alma. To hell with Monk. I don't have to let the police know. They're bound to grab him within a few days, anyway. Leave him out. But we've got to get rid of that lousy money. Won't you try to understand? Once we're rid of it we're in the clear. Getting rid of it is proof neither you nor I tried to steal the stuff. It's off our backs. Then—even if anything ever does come out the police might just give us a break."

"A break! A lot you know. You're crazy."

"If you love me, I'm asking you to do as I say. Please."

"And lose all that money?"

"Alma, we'll manage. Trust me. I can ship that money direct to the newspaper editor of the 'Dispatch' in Boone. We don't need that money. You told me you had a thousand or so of your own—"

"I have. But—"

"When we're married I won't be ashamed to use your money for a week or so until I get a job."

"You fool!" she said furiously. "If you want to know, I'll tell you. I won't let you take that hundred grand from me. I'll kill myself, first!"

"Either we ship that money to Boone or I'm going to the police, Alma. Maybe we should have gone to the police sooner."

She stood, dripping, grasped at the shower pipe, and stepped on to the wet concrete flooring. "Are you insane?"

"I'd stand by you. There ought to be mercy and justice," he said, awkwardly, having to think out the words, "for—people like us—who aren't important. If we confess—and give all the money back we've got—I don't think we'd have to stand too big of a rap. It would wipe our slate clean."

"You wouldn't dare!"

"I'm serious."

"I'd run away. You'd never see me. I thought you loved me so much?"

"I love you so much I want us to have clean slates. You'd be found in a few hours if you tried to run. I'm thinking," he said, "for us both. I'm trying like hell to, anyway, Alma. My father was somebody to be proud of. I'm going to be like him if I can. I'm going to marry you. We're going to have everything that means any thing—love—children, I hope—"

She struck him in the face with the flat of her hand.

"You fool! You fool! Go to the police. You wouldn't dare! You're in this as deep as I am. Go on!" she raged. "Go to the damn coppers."

"All right."

He walked out. He unlocked the cottage door, shut it, walked around the dusty little Hillman, past the acacias blowing raggedly in a soft mountain wind, and around the weedy rock garden with the other little dingy cottages on either side of him. He passed through the entrance to the road and looked back. Then he began walking toward town. The mountain sunshine had a clear brightness. There was a fragrance in the air from spring flowers. He looked back a second time, half expecting to see Alma running after him after having hastily thrown something on. The highway was empty. She hadn't followed him.

He was farther from the center of town than he realized. The cottage camp was at least a mile and a quarter west on the road. He let his legs stretch out. He began thinking of what he would say when he found the police station. It was going to be harder to say than he had thought. There had been something miraculous about meeting Alma. It was as if she had been thrown toward him and he to her, fresh and new. But as soon as he had spoken to the police and they had arrested her and him with her, the freshness would begin to vanish. He felt his steps lagging. All the unspoken questions he had never asked her, and now never wanted to ask her, would be answered for him. It would be in the newspapers, no doubt. Strangers would read about her and Monk Anzeiger. Strangers would not know her as he had learned so quickly to know her in these past few strange days when time had ceased somewhat to be counted as hours and minutes. She would be thrown in jail, too, for how long there was no telling. Perhaps a good lawyer could save her by throwing her on the court's mercy. But where could either Alma or himself find the immense sum of money to pay for one of those clever sly lawyers about whom you read so often in newspapers? He should, he thought, have grabbed that leather bag from the table, taken it, and shipped it back to Iowa. It would be better that way. He paused. She would laugh at him when he returned. She was right. He didn't dare go to the cops. What to do? He started forward again, only to stop once more.

"Bill!"

He swung around, startled. He had not heard the little Hillman coast almost silently down the road to him, halting at the curb. Alma was in there, at the wheel. Now she moved away to the other side of the seat, waiting for him. He ran to the road. He saw she was wearing only her coat. Her naked legs ran from the hem of the coat into her sandals. She was crying. "Bill, you win," she said. "We'll go back.

Ship the money to Iowa. If you're going to be that crazy, I'll be crazy, too!"

The leather bag was waiting on the table when once more he closed the front door and locked it. He could hear water dripping from the shower into the old tub. In the dimness, her eyes were nearly a violet. He looked at her and back to the bag and hesitated. She said angrily, "Go on! Look into the bag. It's all there, if that's what you're thinking. I haven't grabbed five or six thousand dollars to stuff into my coat pockets. See yourself!" She moved and threw open the bag for him to see the tightly packed green flat notes. He shut the bag, feeling a kind of good triumph. It was going to work out for them both. It was wrong to have briefly lost hope. They would have a chance.

"I love you, Bill. I care more for you than anything else, even that stupid hateful money. Wait while I dress and I'll go with you."

"No, I'd better ship it myself. It's safer. Besides, I want to get some clean shirts—and stuff. I'll get back here as fast as possible. I'd like to have a bath . . ." He paused. He was not yet accustomed to saying it straight out to her. It was still very new to know she was his. ". . . I'm beginning to want you like hell. After that, we can eat and start driving west."

"I'm starting to want you like hell, too. I won't dress. Hurry."

It was only ten minutes into town by car. He first stopped at a general merchandise store, buying a cheap suitcase, shirts, socks, underwear, jeans, a jacket of the same material, a peaked cap to hide the color of his hair when he went into the bus office, and dark sunglasses. He changed in the men's room.

He had no trouble at all at the Red Line office. They gave him a receipt for the leather bag, wired the tag on the handle, and it was all an ordinary transaction. He might have been expressing a bag filled with old clothing as far as the clerk was concerned.

He walked out into the bright clear sunshine and he wanted to kick his heels and shout for joy. From now on in, everything was going to be the best ever for Alma and himself. The people at Boone would no doubt try to trace the sender after receiving the bag and discovering what was in it. That was a chance that had to be taken. But by tonight Alma and he would be miles to the west of this little mountain town. The express clerk had scarcely noticed him. There had been four or five people in line behind him, waiting to send their shipments. He had read somewhere it was almost impossible to identify anything printed; and, he had printed the shipping label, instead of writing it in longhand.

The air was so fresh! He saw a yellow-haired girl swinging along toward him and for a startled second thought it was Alma. It wasn't. But he smiled at her and she smiled back at him. He could not wait to get back to Alma. Every girl he saw seemed to remind him of her. A big northbound Red Line bus thundered by and a blonde girl looked at him from the bus window and that was Alma and he lifted his cap and blew her a kiss and laughed at the girl's startled expression. In the parking lot a slim girl in a blue jersey, with bright flaxen hair, was talking to a dark-haired woman. She was Alma. He said, "Hello," and the girl turned. Perhaps there was something so irrepressibly joyous and pleased about him that the slim girl with flaxen hair could not help saying, "Hello, yourself," and laughing because he was laughing.

The Hillman purred all the way on its return. He almost forgot to shut off the engine. He pushed the door; it banged open. Alma had forgotten to lock it. But the bedroom was very still.

"Alma!" he said.

Then he said it again, *"Alma..."*

It was unbelievable. She was gone. She wasn't here. Her suitcase and her coat were gone. The walls of the empty bedroom began closing around him, with the air growing hot and stifling. The bedroom had changed, too. She had taken something from the room with her. He saw what it was.

Half the magazines and old newspapers piled up in one corner of the bedroom had vanished. His heart was like a lump of lead. Had all the magazines and newspapers been there, in that corner, after she had driven to him in the Hillman and he had returned with her to take the leather bag?

He had not then noticed. He had only been thinking of her and of his good triumph in persuading her it was best to ship back the money. He recalled how she had opened the bag for him to see that the money was all there. He had been ashamed of that brief suspicion; he had not even felt down inside the leather bag to be certain it was crammed with packets of money and not—perhaps—two-thirds filled with torn newspapers and torn pages from the magazines. That girl in the Red Line bus to whom he had so gaily blown a kiss? He was struck with more agony of mind. That girl might actually have been Alma. Possibly he had failed to recognize her because the greenish, glare-proof windows in the bus had slightly distorted and magnified the faces looking out into the street.

Now he noticed a scrap of white paper on the floor, near the table. He picked it up. It was a short note she had written him. Evidently she had placed it on the table, expecting him to see it. In opening the door, the mountain breeze had whisked it off the table. Well, that was goddamned thoughtful of her. He had a notion to tear up the note and not read it and he wanted to shout out his anger and bitterness and he walked three times around the room and finally he read what she had written:

Honey:
I've got to get away to think all of this out. If you really love me stay here until Wednesday or Thursday till I have time to sort myself out and decide whether or not we ought to see each other again. I'm not right for you. I shouldn't see you again. If I decide I can't do without you I'll write you from wherever I go. You can decide whether you want to see me, too.

Alma.

He read it a second time. If she had taken most of the money with her, he was thinking angrily, it meant she was planning to get rid of the money before ever writing to him. She would hope she had gulled him. She would possibly even write him. Damn her! Damn her to hell!

She had looked so damned beautiful, too. You could not believe she was really someone like that, ready to twist the heart out of you and having no heart, herself. He wanted to find her and choke her. He would seek her out. He would get back at her, somehow, some way, even if it took him all the rest of—

Someone had entered through the door behind him. A gravelly voice said, "Hello, punk. You didn't know Gramma had Nolly tagging along five or six miles behind in a second car. You wanta watch for things like that, punk. Where is the little bitch?"

Bill got himself around, retreating until the edge of the table cut into the small of his back. Two men had entered. The first was Monk Anzeiger, now wearing a fisherman's sloppy hat, a Norfolk jacket, khaki colored trousers, and old comfortable shoes with rubber soles. Slung over a shoulder was one of those fisherman's wicker baskets or creels, whatever they were called; Bill's mind was having trouble functioning.

Behind Monk was the plump second man, in a very new Norfolk jacket, sporty twill hunting trousers, really the latest thing in sportsmen's moccasins, and a jaunty tweed cap with a feather stuck in the leather band. He was Mr. Nollyfield, the floorwalker in that queer chromium plated Omaha clothing store. You saw him once and ever after he was always the same even if today he had rigged himself in really the jauntiest fisherman's outfit and lacked a carnation for decoration. It was Mr. Nollyfield who closed the door while Monk Anzeiger pointed the short barrelled Colt at Bill and said, "Lemme see that paper you got. Did Alma write where she went?"

Chapter Fifteen

For someone a minute or so ago who had wanted to get back at Alma and had only hatred for her, Bill behaved in the most atrociously unreasonable manner. He had only to give Monk Alma's note, wait, sit tight, and know he had betrayed her as she, he assumed, had betrayed him. However, he did nothing of the sort.

He swung himself to the left of the table, instantly trying to ram the piece of paper in his mouth to get rid of it. Monk was on him. Bill jabbed him, twice, hard lefts to the side of the head, still pushing the piece of paper with his right to his mouth.

But Monk had grabbed at the right arm. Monk slung the pistol barrel over the side of Bill's head, taking Bill's two lefts at the same time. A chair crashed. Bill felt his right arm wrenched harder. The whole room seemed to swim. A crash of steel had blazed a redness before his eyes. Somewhere Nollyfield was shouting in a high-pitched shout.

If he could only get his goddamn hand to his mouth to rip and chew the goddamn note. Monk was slashing again with the pistol barrel. He bore down with all his weight on Bill's right arm. It was almost a stand off for a second or so. Bill was still trying to slug in hard lefts to the jaw and the swarthy cheek. He felt his knuckles crunch under the hard flesh. His right arm was almost immobilized by Monk's left hand gripping it. Monk beat down awkwardly, with his right hand, at Bill's shoulder and face, the steel barrel slashing and slashing. Bill hauled back suddenly. It gave him an instant, with his teeth he snapped at the paper to shred it and destroy it past anyone's attempt to read what Alma had written.

Then it must have been Nollyfield who slithered in behind, gave a loud titter and struck Bill down, gun whipping him. The floor of pine boards tilted up and slammed Bill's face and chest. Someone kicked him in the ribs. After that, everything ended for him.

If he came to in intervals he had no particular awareness; except a dull memory of voices like voices of an old phonograph record. When finally he got back into himself and could look around and know what was happening it must have been night because the naked electric light was glowing, hanging down from the bedroom ceiling. His face felt like an old rubber tire and he found he was slumping in one of the wooden chairs. He was supported there and wrapped around and around with what looked like ordinary sash cords. He had a shock of sorts to see the old snaggly-toothed man in the bedroom. Monk was calling him "Pop" and Monk had a livid welt on his cheek.

Pop said, "Want me to bring food fur him?"

"No," Monk said, "our Willy boy ain't gonna eat yet. You close up your place like we tole you?"

"Sure. Mirandy an' me are keepin' a good watch."

"O.K. Now beat it, Pop."

The old man hesitated at the door. "How long's this goin' to be?"

"What's it to you, Pop? Two hundred on the line, every night. How long do you care?"

"I was jis' askin' . . ." Carrying a tray of empty dishes, the old man closed the door with his foot.

Nollyfield was sitting on the bed, smoking a cigar. He nodded toward Bill and said casually, "Monk, Willy boy's got through sleeping."

Monk lumbered across the room and stared sourly at Bill. "You can save yourself trouble if you know where that little tramp went." He waited. "We read her note. She's gunna be 'round somewhere. Why not spill? We might make it easy on you."

"My dear fellow," said the rather high voice from the bed, "perhaps he doesn't know where our filly's gone?"

"Let's find out. You—you been hittin' that bottle, ain't you?" Monk turned furiously. "I tole you, din't I?"

"I haven't touched a drop," protested Nollyfield. "Hardly a drop."

"You know what I tole you. No drinkin' till we get outa this."

"Of course, Monk. Certainly. Yes, indeed."

Bill looked out of one good eye and one that was partially closed and saw Monk and Nollyfield. Monk was no more than a thinking animal, running to fat. He was brute and muscle and if you could hold yourself together and not let your numbed mind completely fall away into an emptiness perhaps you could plan and think and reason and even predict what someone such as Monk would do. It was very strange, but of the two of them it was Nollyfield over there, something like a fat puff adder, with the sharp little eyes and the smile like a pink painted smile on a face that was only a round swelling of venom, who was the most dangerous. It was he who was licking his lips and sending darting glances past Monk toward Bill and liking to see Bill tied up.

Bill tugged experimentally at the cords. They were only sash cords but they held him damned tight. He had scant hope for himself. How Nollyfield happened to be here with Monk Anzeiger Bill did not know. There was so much he did not know. How Monk had ever managed to get to Omaha to rejoin Gramma was something else, too, he would never know, never expected to know, and was incurious about it. Oh, God, he thought, just let Alma get away.

In the intervening hours when he had seeped off somewhere in painful blackness, Monk and Nollyfield must have managed to piece the scraps of Alma's note together and read what she had written. He saw now the fragments of paper, there, carefully together, like a jigsaw puzzle completed, on the table. They had found out all she had written.

Monk said hoarsely, "Jist lay off that bottle, Nolly, till we finish," and faced Bill again.

"Oh, yes, yes," said Nollyfield. The high voice was like squirtings of venom in the stifling room.

"Spill it, punk," Monk told Bill. "Lissen. We read that tramp's note to you. You hear? We're gunna wait here the nex' three, four days till she writes you where to meet her. We know she took that dough. It ain't here. You know where she went? Say so, kid. Jist spill. It saves us time. Maybe it won't go so hard on you. What's she to you, huh? She ain't nobody to you. Why front for the doll?"

Bill focused on the man before him, having a momentary wonderment at how Monk had been able to find those fishing clothes. Probably Nollyfield had supplied them. It was unimportant. It was hard to swallow. Monk's gun barrel must have caught Bill across the throat in that roughhouse, whenever it was, hours ago. Alma had run out on him, Bill thought, and had taken the money. What was she to him? He had wanted to get back at her. Now all he wanted was for her to escape Monk and Nollyfield. Nothing else very much counted.

"You got any idea where she went, I'm telling you, lemme have it."

"I don't know," Bill said.

"I'm askin' jist once more."

"I don't know." Bill hesitated. He had not shot Monk when the opportunity had been given him. He said, "I gave you a break, Monk. My turn. Give me one."

"That's your hard luck, punk."

"Thanks," Bill said. He laughed at Monk.

Monk hit him . . .

Then they brought him to, again; and Monk was saying, "What chance you got? Try to be smart. Alma's too good-lookin' not to be noticed. She ain't gunna git so far we can't find her. Look how we nailed you here. All Nolly an' me have to do is travel a coupla towns, ask, 'You see a pretty blonde babe inna Hillman?' and finally we git the jackpot in this town on'y we git here a hour late for Alma. But we go into that office and have a talk to Pop. He shows us the register. Ain't you bright? 'Mr. an' Mrs. William Owens, Jr.' on the register. But on'y you are here.

"O.K. I know her. She must be stuck on you to come this far with you and write you that note. Sure. I don't kid myself. She ain't never gone on me. She traveled with me because I could give her dough. Now you ain't gunna spill. That's fine. We can wait. We're gunna roost here. We're gunna roost here till she writes or comes back for her yardy boy an' you ain't gunna eat. Damn you. Steal her from me, will you? You have it good with her, huh?"

Bill didn't answer.

Monk let him have it, maybe two or three times, but with the flat of his hand. The blows stung; they failed to bring oblivion.

"All right," Monk said, turning to Nollyfield. "He don't eat. When he wantsa talk, he eats. Get him into that bathroom. He can't clean outa there."

"Hold it a minute," Nollyfield said.

Nollyfield got himself into the bathroom and Monk worked on Bill a little longer, the big hard flat of the hand being very expert about it. Bill lunged. But the sash cords held, like sharp wires. Nollyfield returned, carrying the brass candle holder with the stump of candle and the matches in the slot. In his new carefully tailored fisherman's getup, Nollyfield wasn't quite real. He gave an affected little laugh. The plump adder's face was rather horrible under the electric shine of light. He indicated the matches stuck in the brass holder.

"We don't want the lad to set fire to himself, do we?"

They cut the cords. Bill made the mistake of trying to fight Monk and Nollyfield. This time Monk threw him to the floor. It was Nollyfield, however, who stepped to him and carefully kicked him between the legs, only once.

There was no pain like that pain, either. Bill writhed, gasped, blacked out, came to, felt himself coming apart, felt them lifting him, throwing him on concrete, heard the bathroom door close, and finally oblivion did mercifully come.

It might have been hours later—he was losing all sense of the flow of time—when he got himself up in the darkness. He stripped, filled the tub, got into the cold water, and the door creaked, a flashlight shining in his face. Again the gravelly voice began asking him about Alma; next, hands pushed his head under the water and he was strangling and his lungs started to burst and he breathed in water.

He knew vaguely he had been lying for some time in the tub, the water drained out of it, with daylight shining dimly through the narrow slit under the roof. It was Tuesday; but whether early morning, late, or around noon, he didn't know. He couldn't see the sun. He got out of the tub. He was very weak. It took him a long time to dress. He heard a mumble of voices from the other room, Monk's, sometimes Nollyfield's, but the men didn't bother him. Once he heard Nollyfield singing, "Down Where the Sunshine Shines." He had quite a voice, too. It carried the tune with a real lilt, every note clear.

Now all Bill could think of or wanted was to have Alma escape these two men. A black horror came on him at the possibility that Alma might return. It would be even worse if she returned instead of writing. How could he signal her before Pop or perhaps that red-headed old woman sucked Alma in with pleasant words? What was there for him to do if she wrote? Monk would intercept the message. Bill dragged himself painfully around the bathroom, going as quietly as possible. Nollyfield was singing again. The lilting innocent words of the tune had an insane quality to them. There was no way out that Bill could see other than by the door into the bedroom. What to do? He couldn't quit. The old dry pine boards forming the outer walls must have been at least half an inch thick. He searched futilely for a weapon.

In the medicine cabinet someone had left a rusted safety-razor on the shelf but there were no blades. A few hairpins were on a lower shelf among a litter of filth, caked dust, an unstopped bottle with the depilatory lotion evaporated into a gummy residue, and an empty box which once had contained face powder and now held dead flies. Along the baseboard he found a single match which must have fallen from the brass candleholder. For a minute or so he had the wild idea of trying to set fire to the bathroom shack. But he would only burn in it while Monk and Nollyfield easily got out of the way of the flames.

He climbed to the cracked toilet seat to stare out through the ventilating opening under the roof. The opening was so narrow and small he had only a restricted view of a field of hay beyond, a glimpse of the road, and a mountain lifting up toward a blue sky. He could get his arm out to signal. But if anyone flashing by in one of those cars half a mile away had even glanced up at the dingy white cottages, among the other equally dingy cottages, they would never have seen the futile waving of an arm.

Sometime that afternoon, or possibly early evening, Pop's voice sounded again in the bedroom. Bill roused himself to listen. A news broadcast had come over Pop's radio. A well known gambler and vice racketeer, Sid Gramellini by name, had been found this afternoon by highway road officers. Apparently he had driven off Spire Rock bridge into the gorge. What had excited Pop was that a half million dollars in new banknotes also had been found in a water-tight metal canister welded underneath the automobile frame. Then, all at once, the voices ceased. Bill heard footsteps leaving the cottage. He waited. They had gone outside, not wanting him to hear.

He had water. He could quench his thirst. That night he heard Nollyfield's voice, arguing with Monk. Spire Rock gorge was only twenty some miles east of town. Pop was beginning to get worried. If the Feds started swarming around that damned smashed Buick and Gramellini's body and the half million from the Boone job, the heat would begin to start burning. How did Monk know that babe was going to show.

Monk's voice said, "Nolly, I tell you I know Alma. I knew her in Chi. Duke Travers brought her there four or five years ago from someplace he'd found her in Pennsy. The punk even married her. When he got the cancer and hadda bust up his band, Alma stuck to the guy even if she coulda had her pick. She kept him going. She got money for his treatments. Duke was a tall blondy sort of bastard, like this country kid. That's the kind she likes. I tell you, she won't be able to stay away. Now, go on. Get the hell outa here and watch the grounds. That hundred grand's mine and yours. Wake me up at four an' I'll take over till daylight . . ."

His consciousness would slip away and he would slump down and come back together again, later; and the same thing would happen all over again. Some time very late, when he believed Monk was asleep, he made a desperate try to break through the door. He knew his strength would be about gone by morning. He got through, too, the door breaking crazily from an upper hinge. But the noise had aroused Monk. Bill stumbled, falling flat. Then Monk was on him, beating him down.

It was hot and still in the bathroom Wednesday. Bill might have lain there, all the time going out. But Monk and Nollyfield carried him to the bedroom. They spilled raw whiskey down his throat. They even fed him food. They got him sitting up and conscious enough to understand they had something for him to read. Monk shoved a post card in his hands. It had arrived this afternoon.

On one side of the card was a highly colored reproduction of a stone gate, and underneath, the caption in small print: "Estes Park Gate. Colorado." He turned it over, having one emotion follow the other. She had loved him enough to write to him! He felt Monk's eyes boring at him. He had the sensation of ice congealing his veins. He read:

Hello, Honey:
Just a couple of lines to tell you I've been seeing the sights. Yesterday I spent 5 hours going thru this crumby park on a bus, trying to make up my mind whether I wanted to see you again. Honey, I decided it just won't ever work out for us. Sorry. I'm on my way to Chi after mailing this. Maybe on to N.Y. to try for a fresh start. Who knows? Don't look for me cause you'll never see me again. I hope this finds you well & safe. But I just had to write before taking the big powder, honey. Good-by.

It wasn't even signed. It did not have to be. He looked at the date marked on the stamp. It had been mailed yesterday, Tuesday, from the town of Estes Park. This was Wednesday. He sat very still on the bed.

He was afraid he'd give it away to Monk by the expression on his face. She had underlined the numeral five and the word "look" in her hastily scribbled note. He remembered how soft and warm and drowsy her voice had been that night they had lain side by side, pleasantly exhausted, in that luxurious lodge outside of Denver. She had wanted to see him again after he had taken his job with the Sacramento newspaper. She would send him a post card, she had said. It would be their secret. He'd know where she would be, to meet her, by the town on the post card. She'd be waiting for him the day after the post card got to him, on the steps of a library because all towns had libraries.

Again he looked at what she had written. Five o'clock, tomorrow, Thursday, she would be on the library steps at the town of Estes Park. She had risked that much. It was all she could do.

Nollyfield's high affected voice said, "That washes it up, Monk. She's bitched him off."

"What do you say, boy? Read it." Monk put on his glasses and his appearance furiously changed. It was like seeing an ape trying to look wise and scholarly and somehow appearing only horribly vacuous. "Did she an' you plan a place to meet in Chi if somethin' went screwy? Give."

After that, it was the same thing, perhaps worse. Bill lay there, half numbed by pain. Let them kill him, just so Alma escaped.

He heard Monk's voice as from very far off, "Lissen, Nolly. I'll get to this Estes Park. Maybe I can pick up her track. I'll hunt down to Denver at the bus stops. She's too good-looking for somebody not to remember. If I don't pick up anything on her there I'll fly north to Cheyenne tonight and try at that end. You keep Will boy till I phone back."

"You aren't too safe, Monk. I'll go. You stay—"

"Lissen. Sure I'm safe. I'm somebody comin' back on a fishin' trip. This moustache'll help. There's a hundred an' fifty million people in the country, ain't there? You get picked off by coppers when you act queer. I been on a lam before, boy. I'll do all right. You stay. The tramp still might double back, trying to be smart with that card."

"I'm telling you. Keep phoning in, Monk."

"Sure. I'll phone in reg'lar. I'll phone tonight from Denver. If nothin's there, I'll phone tomorrow from Cheyenne. Give me three days."

"What about our lad, here?" Nollyfield had been drinking and his voice sounded each syllable distinctly like glass striking glass.

"You know, don't you?"

"Pop and the old harridan?"

"Huh?"

"The old woman—"

"Why not? But wait till I say the word . . ."

They had closed the broken door, pounding nails into the planks laid over the door; and the night wore on.

When Thursday came Bill dragged himself to the tub, filled it, and soaked in the water. That aroused him, some. It was noon, perhaps later. If Monk had managed to locate Alma this morning he would have phoned in with the news, Bill wanted to believe. But the situation seemed unchanged.

It should mean that Monk hadn't yet found her, that he had gone on to Cheyenne, and that Nollyfield was still holding off at this end. In how many more hours would Alma be waiting at some small library's steps?

Bill climbed unsteadily on the toilet seat; once again he tried waving an arm through the ventilating hole. It was of no use. In the distance cars rolled by. None stopped. The sun burnt his skin. He saw dry hay beyond a fence and then he stiffened, clinging with his fingers. The dry grass must have grown very high by now next to the pine boards of this shack. He had once thought of starting a fire—but of starting it from the inside. He had a shower, too. He could turn on the spray of water. It might save him long enough for the blaze outside to burn through the wooden wall.

The match? *Where was it?* It was down under the washbowl where he had let it drop. Feverishly he wadded up the tissue from the roll of toilet paper. The paper caught fire. He stuffed the burning end through the opening, letting the paper unroll. Then he could smell smoke; there was a sudden gushing of heat, a sound of crackling, as dry grass caught. He turned on the spray. Fire burned swiftly in dry grass.

Nollyfield shouted, "Damn you, what are you doing?"

But the boards pounded over the opening of the bathroom door prevented Nolly from getting inside to Bill. Nolly fired. Shots echoed. But Bill crouched down inside the tub, the spray wetting him, fire bright and red through the opening. Smoke was thicker. The old dry planks must have started burning.

From somewhere outside Pop's frightened voice sounded, "It's all on fire. Git some buckets—"

But after that it was very strange because there was only the crackling of fire. All the voices had gone away. The spray of water came down, wetting Bill; but smoke was thick and black now. The heat was intense. If he was going to get through those burning boards it had better be damned quick. Fire scorched his hands. He was coughing. He was too goddamned weak to help himself. There came a splintering. A crowbar thrust through. Somebody outside was spurting water on the fire from a hose. A man got in there and picked up Bill and dragged him through a thin curling redness and away; and the earth seemed to fall apart and next come together again.

Bill dragged himself to his knees, hearing a roaring of blood in his ears. He looked up out of the one eye which was still open.

"I know you, don't I? Aren't you Ed Murvon? Didn't . . . you give me . . ." It was a great effort to get the words out. "You gave me a ride in that souped-up red delivery truck. You're Gramma's partner, aren't you?"

Chapter Sixteen

Ed had said, "This isn't too good for you, Bill. But one won't hurt you. You'll feel rotten afterward, but it'll pick you up for a few hours and I've got to get some sense out of you in a hurry. Drink a lot of water—or beer, if we can find any in this joint. The more liquid you get into your stomach the better. Now, swallow it. Go on."

Bill had hesitated. He realized in a furry dull sort of way that he had gone on making a fool of himself for Ed Murvon had produced a worn leather identification book, with Ed's photograph, and the FBI serial number, and the big seal. He swallowed the rusty colored pill; but he hadn't been able to see that it had picked him up so very much.

In the empty main cottage Ed Murvon found ham and cold beans and bottled beer and made Bill just sit there at the table and eat and drink beer, growling at him, "Go on. Get that beer and food down so that damn pill won't hit you too hard. You're beginning to wake up. You can hear me all right, can't you?"

Yes, Bill could hear him, all right. He didn't know why Ed was asking. Bill could hear fine. He sat there at the table and drank more of the beer and he could see Ed clearly enough from the one eye and there was even a kind of glimmering where the other eye wasn't stuck entirely tight after most of the caked blood had been washed off. But Ed was nuts about that pill. Bill couldn't feel it hitting. He couldn't feel much of anything. He let Ed do the talking while he tried to think why it wasn't all right to sit where he was and not move and let Ed talk. There was something else he must do. Time was running short. He would think of it in a few minutes if he just sat very quietly, waiting for his brains to shape back together again.

Ed said, "I'll give it to you all in one piece to connect together so you can fill in fast. I traced you as far as Omaha, last Saturday. And I lost you in Omaha. The stick-up trail mushed off there, too. So we hashed around. I couldn't get you out of my mind. I even wired Washington to check your father's service record. Washington cleared back to Cedar Rapids and the newspaper and to Sacramento. I began learning about you, Bill. But that didn't tie to the Boone job. Yesterday morning we got a wire from Colorado. Gramellini had been found, smashed inside his smashed car, with half a million in new currency. I was on a plane twenty minutes after the wire hit Omaha."

Ed opened another bottle of beer. "Keep listening. I'm going to need all your help, Bill. My two men are still at the other end of town. Half an hour ago I drove to this camp, saw the fire, jumped out, and recognized Phil Nollinger, or Nollyfield as he likes to call himself. He saw me and got over the fence. I don't know where the old man and woman scattered. There you are. How do you feel? Better? What's Phil Nollinger here for? I've phoned for a pick-up on him. Omaha's blown wide open. They've closed the store after Gramellini's smash-up hit the newspapers. But where do you tie in, Bill? I've got to know that . . ."

Bill slowly began explaining. He could remember, all right. His mind was growing clear enough for that. It was almost like that scopolamine business. Perhaps it was the beer.

Ed had gone to the wall phone, now, giving instructions to someone at the other end of the wires. Bill sat there, listening, the blister on his arm hurting. All of him hurt. Into the phone Ed was saying something about watching Cheyenne, Chicago, and New York airports for Monk Anzeiger. Bill lurched up from the seat. Ed looked around at him.

"Mr. Murvon—"

Ed said, "This kid up here's going to need a doctor. Better send—"

"No—"

"Call you back." Ed hung up.

Bill said, "Alma and I sent the money back. I've got the express receipt to prove it . . ." He broke off. He was remembering everything now. The time! Even now Alma might be waiting for him.

"What time is it?"

Ed gazed a moment at Bill, looked at his watch, said, "Ten after four. Take it easy."

"Alma!"

"Easy, Bill. Where is she?"

"Will you have to arrest her?"

"It looks like it, Bill. You, too, I'm afraid. I'll do all I can for you. I suppose you smashed up Gramellini? You can claim self-defense. But I won't lie to you. You and this girl—"

"She'll be waiting for me at five. Let me go to her. Let me just talk to her a minute or so and be with her and explain. Then you can take us. We aren't running. Both Alma and I are through running. We even tried to send back the hundred thousand. We both wanted clean slates."

"All right, Bill," he said quietly. "I think your father paid high enough of a price to his country to earn his son a few breaks. Let me just call through once more."

This time Ed didn't have his red delivery truck. He was driving an old Chevy and Bill wished they were back in that souped-up delivery truck because it would have gone faster over the mountain highway toward the town of Estes Park. It was forty-two miles, and Bill didn't think they would get there by five. He was afraid Alma might not wait many minutes for him. She would be nervous and jumpy. Even loving her as he did, he could not help by now knowing a little how she was. She didn't have very much courage. She broke too easily. She was inclined to run.

On the way Ed's voice asked more questions. Bill answered. Gradually, Ed said, he could begin piecing together what had happened to Bill or at least most of it.

Bill said, "I lied to you about one thing, Mr. Murvon."

"Did you? Why not call me 'Ed?'"

"I thought I was shipping back all the money."

"You took the bag to the express office."

"Yes, I did." Bill heard the big rushing sound of the Chewy slamming around a wall of rock. The valley below was all green and cut up with black lines, like a checkerboard, where drainage ditches had been dug.

"Alma?" said Ed.

"Alma stuffed some of the money in the bag, Ed. But I'm afraid she filled up most of the bag with newspapers. It was too much for her to give up all at once. She *did* write me. She is waiting for me. Doesn't that prove she's ready to send back every rotten penny? Are Alma and I going to have . . ."

He could not finish. He did not care about himself. Alma! She might die in jail. It would change her. She would never be the same. All he was asking was for their one chance to wipe the slate clean.

"I don't know what to tell you, Bill. I've been worrying about you. I learned about that uncle of yours. You've had bad breaks since your father and mother died. I'd even thought you might like coming out with my wife and me to our pear ranch. We never had any kids. But this girl . . ."

"I don't want to know about her. I'm in love with her. She's in love with me. That's all that's important."

Ed never said anything. He tooled the Chevy around a mountain curve.

"Why don't people do something?" Bill said.

"Do something?"

"Against Gramellini," Bill said. "Against all of them like Gramellini. It's in the newspaper every day. Nobody cares."

"I won't believe the nation's gone rotten because of the bad apples. I know quite a lot about you, Bill. You're going to be all right. But that girl—"

"Meet her first before you say anything against her. She does want a chance, Ed."

"I don't know what to say . . ." Ed ceased speaking a minute. The Chevy was laboring up a long climb. "Bill, I got a funny mind. I wouldn't have been so long on this job, if I hadn't. Something just came to me. You skipped too fast over that scopolamine nastiness. Gramellini knew you'd meet Alma at the Omaha library. You told him. All right. But Nollinger—Nollyfield, as you know him—he was there that time, wasn't he? *He* knew that deal you and Alma worked out to meet in a strange town at a library. Wouldn't he have told Monk? Suppose Monk's decided to make this a four-way cross to improve on Gramellini's triple-cross? *Suppose he's waiting at the library, believing Alma just might show up?* It wouldn't have been too hard for him to've faked phoning to Nollyfield, saying he was on his way to Denver."

Suppose Monk was? What time was it? Ten minutes of five. There were still twelve more miles. In his mind's eye he could see Alma walking toward the steps, perhaps even now. If Monk was somewhere near, in a cigar store, a shoe store, a tourist novelty shop, watching and watching, all these hours! Even if it was a corkscrew road, Ed ceased trying to drive with reasonable caution. They got into the town at three minutes, precisely, after five. But they lost wretched minutes trying to find someone who knew where the library was. Then a boy at the third gas station did know. It was two blocks west. It wasn't much of a place. You had to look for it or you'd drive by.

It wasn't much of a place, either. Alma was not yet there. Ed stopped on the far corner. Bill said, "Let me wait for her. I *know* she'll come. Just give me a few minutes to get her ready."

"Hold it—" Ed got out of the car, sighting around. It was another afternoon that couldn't be better. Three women walked by in bright cottons. "It looks like I was wrong about Monk Anzeiger trying to stash himself out. Anyway, I'll have a prowl into these stores. Get across the street. Keep your eyes sharp. If you see him, start yelling and keep yelling."

It was a drowsy afternoon, very much like that drowsy Sunday afternoon back in a little town of western Nebraska. A tourist bus drove by. The flowers in the garden were yellow and red. Bill felt foolish for having frightened himself. Monk would be hundreds of miles away. He waited. He began to be afraid Alma had changed her mind and perhaps, by now, she, too, was somewhere miles and miles away. Then he caught sight of her and his heart leaped. She was wearing a new print dress with a foolishly lovely wide straw hat on her head and she was carrying the heavy leather bag. She came around the corner of the street all of a sudden, as if she had materialized out of nothing to stand in front of the library and smile at him.

"Bill—"

"Alma—"

"I tried to run away from you and couldn't. Don't be sore at me."

"You took the money—"

"Yes. You found that out? I don't terribly care. You can ship it back. I just want you. I was afraid you wouldn't be staying in that crumby cottage camp to get my post card. Oh, Bill, I'm so glad to see you."

She had run off because she had not wanted to lose the money. She had tried to run away from Bill; and she had found she could not. With a strange feeling of his heart all at once losing all the leaden heaviness, Bill reached down for the shabby leather bag. He had been so much afraid that Alma and he never would have a chance to begin all over, fresh, again, with a clean slate. He had thought it was too late. It wasn't. They were going to have their chance! It was not too late after all.

"Let's get out of here, Alma. There's a lot to tell—"

"Bill!" That was Ed shouting a frantic warning from across the street.

Bill whirled around. The bag fell to the pavement, the old leather splitting. Someone else was speaking down to Bill, higher up on the library steps. Monk Anzeiger was there, inside the open library door.

"All right, you tramp. Here's where your boy gets it and you—"

Monk shot twice. Ed was shooting from across the street. But Alma had taken both of Monk's shots, flinging herself in front of Bill. He held her. Somehow Monk went tumbling down the steps to sprawl in a heap on the hot pavement. People were shouting. Bill held tightly to Alma, refusing to believe it. Her eyes opened.

"Bill, dear," she whispered. "Find some nice girl . . . I'm glad . . ."

Because a great deal of fresh crisp money had been spilled on the street around a dead girl, a boy who seemed turned to stone, and a dead man, the two local police were having trouble with the crowd. Ed was speaking very loudly but Bill didn't hear him.

Men in quiet gray and brown suits had arrived in another car. There followed a senseless whirling of many voices. A robin flew to the branch of a tree and sang three clear notes and flew away again.

In the Chevy now, Ed was saying in a queer harsh way as if he had a fishbone in his throat, "I'll see you through, Bill."

It was hard to believe. The sky was still blue, as blue as her eyes. Nothing had changed. He could breathe. He was alive. It hadn't happened. He had not fought and raged to go with her in that dusty white ambulance to wherever she would be taken.

It was all right, he told himself. It was the heat and the humidity. He'd be fine in a few minutes. He would see her again, somewhere, sometime, someday. "Hello, Bill," she would say. "Hello, Alma," he would say.

He had wanted to die with her. Alma! Alma! There had never really been any chance for either of them. He knew now he always had known. She must have, too. Even so, she had tried to return to him. She had tried to return, he thought. She had been ready to send back the money. He felt the dusty pain taking him. He had to hold on. In another minute, if he didn't, he was going to break apart and crumple and split into fragments.

Ed's voice was saying, "We'll manage, Bill. I'll stick by you. She didn't fail you in the end. Always remember that. She didn't fail you. She'd want you to look ahead. There'll be good years." Ed's voice was shaking. "You're young, yet."

All Bill's youth had been wiped out in that one crimson second. He felt it take her and take him. Alma! The girl he loved had loved him enough at the last moment to spare him from the hard quick death. He could look ahead. There might be good years or bad years; he didn't know. All he now knew was that he was unendurably alone, that Alma was gone, and that with her going all the bright promise of being young had gone, too.

THE END

DARWIN TEILHET BIBLIOGRAPHY
(1904-1964)

Novels
Murder in the Air (1931)
Death Flies High (1931)
The Talking Sparrow Murders (1934)
Bright Destination (1935)
The Ticking Terror Murders (1935)
The Crimson Hair Murders (1936; with Hildegarde Teilhet)
The Feather Cloak Murders (1936; with Hildegarde Teilhet)
Journey to the West (1938)
The Broken Face Murders (1940; with Hildegarde Teilhet)
Trouble Is My Master (1942)
Retreat From the Dolphin (1943)
Odd Man Pays (1944)
My True Love (1945)
The Fear Makers (1945)
Something Wonderful to Happen (1947)
The Happy Island (1950)
The Mission of Jeffery Tolamy (1951)
The Marble Forest (1951; as Theo Durant; a round robin mystery featuring 12 authors)
Steamboat on the River (1952)
The Lion's Skin (1955)
The Road to Glory (1956)
The Big Runaround (1964; reprinted as *Dangerous Encounter*, 1967)

As William H. Fielding
The Unpossessed (1951)
Take Me As I Am (1952)
Beautiful Humbug (1954)

As Cyrus Fisher
The Avion My Uncle Flew (1946)
Ab Carmody's Treasure: Mystery and Adventure in Guatemala (1948; as Cyrus T. Fisher)
The Hawaiian Sword (1956; as Cyrus T. Fisher)

Selected filmography (source writer)
They Wanted to Marry (1937; from a short story)
No Room for the Groom (1952; from the novel, *My True Love*)
The Fearmakers (1958), from the novel, *The Fear Makers*)

Darwin LeOra Teilhet was born May 20, 1904 in Wyanet, Illinois. As a teenager, he traveled in France and worked as a juggler in a circus. He went on to write a monthly column on broadcast radio for *Forum* magazine from  1932 to 1934, and performed intelligence work during World War II. Teilhet later became executive assistant to the president of Dole Pineapple in Hawaii, taught journalism at Stanford, and worked as a screenwriter. Teilhet published his first mystery in 1931, *Murder in the Air*, and went on to write several novels featuring detective Baron von Kaz, three of them with his wife Hildegarde. He also used the pseudonyms Cyrus Fisher (young adult novels, one of which won the Newbery Honor award) and William H. Fielding (crime thrillers for Gold Medal Books). Teilhet died April 18, 1964, in Palo Alto, California.

Black Gat Books is new line of mass market paperbacks introduced in 2015 by Stark House Press. New titles appear every month, featuring the best in crime fiction reprints. Each book is size to 4.25" x 7", just like they used to be. Collect them all.

Harry Whittington · Haven for the Damned #01
Charlie Stella · Eddie's World #02
Leigh Brackett · Stranger at Home #03
John Flagg · The Persian Cat #04
Gary Phillips · Only the Wicked #05
Malcolm Braly · Felony Tank #06
Vin Packer · The Girl on the Bestseller List #07
Orrie Hitt · She Got What She Wanted #08
Helen Nielsen · The Woman on the Roof · #09
Lou Cameron · Angel's Flight #10
Gary Lovisi · The Affair of Lady Westcott's #11
Arnold Hano · The Last Notch #12
Clifton Adams · Never Say No to a Killer #13
Ed Lacy · The Men from the Boys #14
Henry Kane · Frenzy of Evil #15
William Ard · You'll Get Yours #16
Dolores & Bert Hitchens · End of the Line #17
Noël Calef · Frantic #18
Ovid Demaris · The Hoods Take Over #19
Fredric Brown · Madball #20
Louis Malley · Stool Pigeon #21
Frank Kane · The Living End #22
Ferguson Findley · My Old Man's Badge #23
Paul Connelly · Tears Are For Angels #24
E. P. Fenwick · Two Names for Death #25
Lorenz Heller · Dead Wrong #26
Robert Martin · Little Sister #27
Calvin Clements · Satan Takes the Helm #28
Jack Karney · Cut Me In #29
George Benet · Hoodlums #30
Jonathan Craig · So Young, So Wicked #31
Edna Sherry · Tears of Jessie Hewett #32
William O'Farrell · Repeat Performance #33
Marvin Albert · the Girl With No Place to Hide #34
Edward Aarons · Gang Rumble #35
William Fuller · Back Country #36
Robert Silverberg · Killer #37
William R. Cox · Make My Coffin Strong #38
A. S. Fleischman · Blood Alley #39
Harold R. Daniels · The Girl in 304 #40
William H. Durhart · The Deadly Pay-Off #41
William Ames · Awake and Die #42
Charles Runyon · Object of Lust #43
Dr. Gatskills Blue Shoes · Paul Conant #44

Stark House Press
1315 H Street, Eureka, CA 95501 (707) 498-3135
griffinskye3@sbcglobal.net www.starkhousepress.com
Available from your local bookstore or direct from the publisher

www.ingramcontent.com/pod-product-compliance
Lightning Source LLC
LaVergne TN
LVHW021811060526
838201LV00058B/3333